A SPANISH
HONEYMOON

A SPANISH HONEYMOON

BY

ANNE WEALE

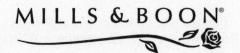

MILLS & BOON®

First published in Great Britain 2002
Large Print edition 2002
Harlequin Mills & Boon Limited,
Eton House, 18-24 Paradise Road,
Richmond, Surrey TW9 1SR

© Anne Weale 2002

ISBN 0 263 17343 7

Set in Times Roman 16 on 16½ pt.
16-0702-60328

Printed and bound in Great Britain
by Antony Rowe Ltd, Chippenham, Wiltshire

CHAPTER ONE

La mujer sin hombre es como el fuego sin leña.

Woman without man is like fire without wood.

THERE were nights when Liz couldn't sleep.

Memories...regrets...doubts...unfulfilled longings...elation at breaking free...panic at her recklessness; all these fizzed about in her brain, like the firecrackers the village boys let off in the street on *fiestas*, and made sleeping impossible.

When this happened she would get out of bed, make a mug of herb tea and, unless it was raining, which was blessedly seldom in this benign climate, climb the outside staircase to the flat roof where she dried her laundry and sunbathed.

One night she was up there, gazing at the moonlit mountains surrounding the valley, when she was startled by noises. They came from the big house that had its front door on the next street up the hillside on which the small Spanish village of Valdecarrasca was built.

5

Named after the fig tree in a corner of its walled garden, the big house was called La Higuera. Its rear windows overlooked the roof-tops of the terrace of much smaller houses on the street below, where Liz lived. But as La Higuera had been empty since her arrival, six months ago, she had almost forgotten that, some day, its owner would return and her flat roof would no longer be as private as it had been up to now.

The first intimation that someone had arrived was the rattling sound of the *persianas* being rolled up, releasing a glow of light from each of the ground-floor windows.

Liz's instinctive reaction was to leap up from the lounger, hurry down the staircase and dis-appear into her house before anyone at La Higuera noticed her.

Standing in her unlighted kitchen, she waited to see if the blinds hiding the upstairs windows of the big house would be rolled up. It might not be Cameron Fielding, the owner, who had arrived. Sometimes, she had been told, he lent the house to his friends.

To many of the foreigners living in or around the village, Cameron Fielding was a household name. Liz had never heard of him until she started living in Valdecarrasca. Nor, from what she had been told, did she like the sound of him.

However, being a fair-minded person, she took some of the more scandalous stories with a pinch of salt.

Whoever it was who had arrived at La Higuera must have come without Alicia being notified, she thought, as she watched and waited.

Alicia was the portly Spanish lady paid a retainer to keep an eye on the house while it was empty, and to air and clean it before anyone used it. According to village rumour, she was supposed to do this once a month so that it was always in order. In practice, so Liz had heard, she did it only a day or two before Mr Fielding or his guests were expected.

This time, it seemed, she had been caught napping. To Liz's certain knowledge, Alicia had not set foot in the place for months, which meant that every horizontal surface would be thick with dust and the rooms would have a musty smell.

Wondering if tomorrow Alicia would find herself out on her ear, Liz saw one of the upstairs *persianas* being hauled up by the stout tape that reeled the slats into a box at the top of the window. Many village houses, including her own, still had the old-fashioned wooden-slatted blinds that were pulled up by cords into a roll that remained visible. But La Higuera had been altered and modernised.

The person who had lifted the blind was a man but, because he was silhouetted by the lights in the room behind him, all she could see was that he was tall and broad-shouldered, with dark hair. In fact he looked like a Spaniard. Although many of the elderly locals were short and often bandy-legged, owing to an inadequate diet in the years when Spain was a poor and backward country, the younger Spaniards had much better physiques and were as well-built as their contemporaries in other parts of Europe.

Then a second person came into view, a woman. As the man, whoever he was, stood looking out at the moonlit valley, she moved close behind him and put her arms round him. Immediately he swung round to return her embrace. Liz saw his head bend towards the girl's and, for quite a long time, they engaged in what was clearly a passionate kiss.

It was still going on when, almost as if some sixth sense told him they were not as private as they might expect to be in a small Spanish village at one o'clock in the morning, he reached out an arm towards the side of the window. The next moment Liz's view of the embrace was blocked by the pair of curtains whose draw-cord he must have pulled.

Feeling as guilty as if she had been caught watching something far more intimate than a kiss, Liz drew the kitchen curtains and felt her way to the light switch. Then she made another cup of tea and took it up to her bedroom, intending to continue reading the book on top of the stack on her night table.

But, like a love scene in a movie or on TV, what she had seen had stirred up the powerful yearnings that, as they had no hope of being realised, she did her best to keep battened down.

She was also curious to know if the man in the bedroom at La Higuera was, in fact, the legendary womaniser whose amorous exploits provided so many titbits of gossip for his fellow foreigners to relish.

'…a different girlfriend every time he comes here,' was one of the allegations Liz had heard about him.

'Not what you could call handsome, but *madly* attractive…my goodness, yes, as attractive as the devil and *totally* without morals. Still, as he isn't married, can you blame him for grabbing his opportunities?' was another comment that had stuck in her memory.

Liz, who had had her childhood and teenage years blighted by a man of the same stamp who *had* been married, was disposed to dislike all philanderers. She had no time for people who treated sex as a game. She despised them all.

Despite a disturbed night, she was up at her usual early hour the next day. Brushing her teeth in the bathroom, she thought for the umpteenth time how different she looked today from the way she had looked on arrival, pallid-faced and drawn after a cold and wet northern European winter and a succession of head colds caught while commuting from her home in the outer suburbs to her workplace in central London.

Now, even after a disturbed night, she had three times as much vitality as she had ever had in England. She had never been a beauty. Her dark blue eyes and her clear skin—once pale but now lightly tanned—were her best features, counterbalanced by a disastrous nose and a rather unfeminine chin.

In her other life, as she had begun to think of it, she had adapted her hairstyle to a conservative version of whatever was the prevailing fashion. Here, to save money, she had given up going to the hairdresser and let it grow to a length she could tie back or pin up. Her basic colour was mid-brown. In place of professionally-done highlights, these days she had only sun streaks, helped by rubbing selected strands with a cut lemon. There was always a lemon to hand because there was a *limonero*, that bore fruit all year round, growing in her little back yard.

After a quick hot shower, she dressed in a plain white T-shirt, a navy blue cotton skirt and navy sneakers. Later she was driving to the weekly produce market in a larger village a few kilometres away. She had planned, immediately after breakfast, to spend half an hour working in the walled garden of La Higuera.

In the same way that Alicia was supposed to look after the interior of the house, the previous owner of Liz's house, an elderly Englishwoman called Beatrice Maybury, had undertaken to take care of the neighbouring garden. Beatrice had asked if Liz would be willing to continue this work and Liz had agreed. She had always liked gardening, and the generous fee paid to her predecessor in return for an hour's work a week would be a welcome addition to her limited funds. At that time, of course, she had not known the kind of man the house belonged to. Beatrice had never mentioned his predatory tendencies. Perhaps she had been unaware of them since, by all accounts, she had kept herself to herself and not been part of the expatriates' grapevine.

After their late arrival, and whatever had followed that passionate kiss, it seemed unlikely the people staying at La Higuera would be up and about before mid-morning. Liz decided to stick to her plan and do some weeding and watering before they surfaced for the day.

She entered the property by a gate at the side of the house that, by way of a narrow passage, led down to the 'secret' garden at the rear. Most of the larger houses in the main part of the village did not have gardens, only patios. In the rest of Europe, a patio meant any paved sitting-out area. But in Spain it was an open area within the structure of a building. In Valdecarrasca, many of the houses too small to have a patio had a small garden or yard. But the garden behind La Higuera was the size of a tennis court.

Her first task today was to plant out some cuttings she had taken from a clump of silvery-grey artemisia and kept, in water, in a dark green wine bottle until they put out small roots.

She was on her knees by the narrow bed at the foot of the wall clad with variegated ivy that spilled over the top and cascaded into her own little yard on the other side, when a man's voice said, 'Hello...who are you?'

The question gave Liz such a start that she let out a muffled squeak and, in scrambling to her feet, almost overbalanced. He stepped forward, grabbing her arm to steady her.

'Sorry...I didn't mean to scare you. I suppose you thought the house was still empty. I got back late last night, or rather early this morning. I'm Cam Fielding, the owner. And you are…?'

She had known who he was immediately. 'Madly attractive' had not been an exaggeration. He was unquestionably the most attractive man she had ever encountered.

Last night she had taken him for a Spaniard and he did have some of their characteristics: the black hair and eyebrows, the olive skin that tanned easily, and the hawk-like features that often indicated Moorish ancestry. But although by no means all Spanish people had brown eyes, she had yet to meet one whose irises were the colour of steel.

'I'm Liz Harris,' she said, acutely aware of his grip on her arm and also of the fact that, under a white terry bathrobe, he was undoubtedly naked. Glancing downwards, she saw that his feet were bare, which was why she hadn't heard him approaching. Looking up again, she noticed his hair was damp. He must have just had a shower, come downstairs to make coffee and seen her from the kitchen window.

She had never been inside his house but Beatrice had described its layout so she knew that the two doors set close to each other led into the kitchen and the garage.

'Are you Mrs Harris's daughter…or her daughter-in-law?' he asked.

'Neither…I'm Mrs Harris.' She wished he would let go of her arm and move back a bit. At such close quarters his physical magnetism was uncomfortably strong.

He lifted an eyebrow. 'I see. I expected you to be much older…the same age as Beatrice Maybury. When she wrote that an English widow was buying her cottage, I assumed that you were contemporaries. How old are you?'

'Thirty-six,' said Liz, relieved that he had finally let go of her arm so that she could step back and widen the distance between them. It was rather a cheek to ask her age at this early stage of their acquaintance, she thought. 'How old are you?' she countered.

'Thirty-nine,' he replied. 'Was your husband much older than you…or did he die untimely young?'

'He was a year older. He died four years ago.' She had never met anyone who asked such personal questions so soon. Most people carefully avoided mentioning anything to do with her premature widowhood.

'What happened?'

'He was drowned trying to rescue a child in a rough sea. He wasn't a very good swimmer. They were both lost,' Liz answered flatly. Duncan's heroism was still a puzzle to her. He had been a cautious man, not one who took risks or chances. The courage and folly of his last act had been totally out of character.

'That makes his action even braver,' said Fielding. 'Were you living in Spain when it happened?'

'No, in England. We had stayed in Spain several times with his parents. They used to rent a villa to escape the worst of the winter. But I like the mountains better than the seaside resorts. Beatrice Maybury's brother—the one she's gone back to look after—knows my father-in-law. Mr Maybury thought my parents-in-law might like to buy her house. I came out with them to look at it. They didn't like it, but I did.'

'And how is it working out?' Fielding asked. 'The majority of the British expats in this part of Spain are retired…though the number of young working expats is building up, so I'm told. Do you have a job apart from keeping this garden in order?'

'I'm a freelance needlework designer… mainly for women's magazines. It's work I can do anywhere—thanks to e-mail.'

Her attention was distracted by colour and movement on the terrace built out from the house. The girl she had seen last night was coming to join them. Like Fielding, she was wearing a robe, but his was utilitarian and hers was designed to be more decorative than practical.

Made of irregular layers of chiffon in sunset colours, it floated, cloud-like, round a spectacular figure of the kind displayed at movie premières and Oscar presentations.

'Cam...the fridge is empty. There's no orange juice,' this vision said plaintively, wafting down the steps that connected the terrace and garden.

'I know. I'll get some from the shop. I didn't expect you to get up until later.' He introduced them. 'Mrs Harris...this is my house guest, Fiona Lincoln. Fiona, this is my neighbour from over the wall. Mrs Harris keeps the garden in order.'

Liz removed the cotton gardening glove from her right hand. She was not surprised to find that Fiona had a limp handshake. She didn't look the sort of person who would shake hands firmly. Glamorous women hardly ever did, in Liz's experience. Perhaps they thought it was unfeminine to exert any pressure.

'I thought you had a maid to look after things,' Fiona said to Cam.

Despite not being dressed for the day, she was already fully made up, Liz noticed.

'I have a cleaning lady, but it doesn't look as if she's been in recently,' he answered. 'Do you know my home help, Mrs Harris? Is she ill or something?'

'Beatrice mentioned that you had help... someone called Alicia. But we don't run into each other,' Liz told him. 'I'm usually here before breakfast or in the late afternoon. I expect she comes in the middle of the day.'

'I know where she lives. I'll call round there. Now we'll leave you in peace while we get ourselves organised. Catch you later.' As they turned away, he put a possessive hand on the other woman's slender waist.

Watching Fiona leaning against him as far as the foot of the steps, Liz felt a moment of envy. She would have given a lot to have a man in her life against whom she could lean like that. At the same time she knew that a relationship such as theirs—she felt sure it wasn't 'serious' and would probably end as casually as it had begun—would not satisfy her. She could never take a lover purely for physical pleasure, or be a temporary girlfriend.

The stairs to the terrace were narrow, with succulents growing in clay pots placed at the outer edge of each tread. Before mounting them, Fiona furled her floating layers of chiffon, wrapping the garment more closely around her and, in so doing, drawing Fielding's attention to the curves of her shapely bottom.

Watching him admiring it, Liz wondered how men like him and her father could be satisfied with making love to women for whom they felt no real affection or even liking. To her, the idea of going to bed with someone you didn't love was repugnant.

Because she had married so young, she had missed the sexual freedom enjoyed by most of her generation. Duncan had been her first boy-friend and her only lover. That she might marry again seemed doubtful. Unattached men of the right age were thin on the ground. And anyway did she want to marry a second time? Marriage was such a huge risk.

With a sigh, she resumed her planting.

After lunch, Liz went for a walk on the dirt lanes and narrow tarmacked roads criss-crossing the vineyards that stretched from the edge of the village to the far side of the valley. When she arrived the grapes had been tiny, no larger than orange pips. She had seen them grow and ripen until they were ready to be picked. Now the vine leaves were turning red or purple.

On the way back, she followed a lane that gave her an overall view of Valdecarrasca. Its clustered rooftops were dominated by the church and a sloping line of cypress trees lead-ing up to the small white-walled cemetery where coffins were placed in banks of narrow vaults marked by their occupants' photographs as well as their names and dates.

Even for an outsider, it was a comfortable feeling to be part of a small close-knit community where each generation had been at school together and had many shared memories.

The rest of the afternoon was spent working on a design for a tablecloth and matching napkins for a 'garden lunch' feature scheduled for publication the following summer.

At six o'clock she went downstairs to fix herself a gin and tonic and started preparing the salad she would eat at seven. Some of the foreigners who lived here had adapted to Spanish meal times and had a *siesta* after lunch. For the time being, in her own home, she was sticking to the timetable she had always been used to.

She was about to halve one of the avocado pears that were so much cheaper here than in London, when someone knocked on her front door. To her surprise, when she opened it, she found Cameron Fielding standing on the narrow pavement outside.

'I hope this isn't an inconvenient moment to call. Do you have five minutes to spare?'

'Of course. Come in.'

She stood back while he ducked his head to avoid cracking it on the rather low lintel. Two of the things that had put her parents-in-law off the house were the absence of a hall and the lack of light in the room facing the street. It only had one small window guarded by an iron *reja* as was standard in Spanish houses whether they were palaces or cottages.

'Come through to the kitchen,' she said, after closing the door.

Fielding waited for her to lead the way. Perhaps it was the first time he had been here, she thought. Because Beatrice had been to his house it didn't mean he had been to hers.

But a moment later he corrected this assumption by saying, 'You've had the kitchen altered. It's much better now…much lighter.'

'Beatrice wasn't keen on cooking. I enjoy it,' said Liz. 'I'm having a *gin-tonic*.' This, she had read, was what trendy young Spaniards called what her parents called a G and T. 'Can I offer you one?'

'Thank you. Ice but no lemon, please.'

Liz fixed the drink and, with a gesture, waved him to the basket chair in the corner. 'What did you want to see me about?'

'I've always suspected that not a lot of cleaning went on when I wasn't around. This unexpected visit has confirmed it. The house obviously hasn't been touched since the last time I was here.' His powerful shoulders lifted in a philosophical shrug. 'Well, that's not unusual. It happens in lots of countries where foreigners have vacation houses. Incomers are usually re-garded as suckers with more money than sense. Cheers!' He raised his glass to her.

'Cheers!' she echoed. Was he going to ask her to take on the housework as well as the gar-den? Surely not.

'Alicia is not a bad worker when she gets down to it, but she needs keeping an eye on,' he went on. 'I was wondering if you would be willing to provide that supervision...to make sure she does what she's supposed to do. Also I'd like to have someone I can rely on to stock the fridge and maybe arrange some flowers. But perhaps you're far too busy with your own work to tackle anything more?'

Liz had been preparing a frosty answer if he asked her to take over the cleaning. Not because she considered housework beneath her, but be-cause she resented him thinking her own work was little more than a hobby.

While she was rethinking what she had in-tended to say, he went on, 'By the way, it's obvious that you're doing far more in the garden than Beatrice did. I don't think I'm paying you enough. If you were willing to oversee Alicia's work, I'd be happy to increase your fee.'

He then suggested an amount, in pesetas. It seemed such a massive increase that, at first, Liz

thought she must have made a mistake convert-
ing it into pounds. Even after six months here,
she still tended to think in sterling except with
small everyday transactions.

'If you feel that isn't enough, I'm open to
negotiation,' he said, watching her with those
curiously penetrating grey eyes.

'It's enough…more than enough. But I need
time to think it over. I'm not sure I want to take
on the double commitment. For one thing, my
Spanish is still pretty basic. I get by with the
man at the bank who comes from away, but the
village people seem to have a problem with my
accent. Do you speak Spanish?'

He nodded. 'Try out your Spanish on me.' He
suggested some sentences for her to translate
and, when she had done her best with them,
said, 'You're coming along very well. Remember that the people here speak Valenciano, the
regional language, from choice and Castilian
Spanish to communicate with outsiders.
Nowadays, with supermarkets everywhere, the
expats who live near the coast can get by without learning any Spanish, and most of them do.'

'How did you learn the language?'

'My grandparents retired here after spending
most of their lives abroad. My parents were also
abroad a lot and I used to come here during the

school holidays. Children pick up languages faster than adults do.'

'Was La Higuera your grandparents' house?'

'No, they lived on the coast, before it became overcrowded. When my grandfather died, he left their house to me. But by then it was surrounded by elaborate ''villas'' with swimming-pools, so I sold it and bought La Higuera for when I retire.'

Liz picked up the critical note in his voice. 'What have you got against swimming-pools?' she asked.

'In a country like this, with a chronic shortage of water, they're an unsustainable extravagance. The main blame lies with the planners who, up to now, haven't introduced legislation to make it obligatory for all new houses to have *cisternas* filled by rainwater, not mains water. People without *cisternas* should swim in the sea, or have very small exercise pools and swim against power-jets.' He finished his drink and stood up. 'We're here until Saturday evening. When you make up your mind, call me. The number is in the book.'

She saw him out. Returning to the kitchen, she was uncomfortably conscious that she would have liked him to stay longer. Yet, apart from his looks and his charm, what did he have to recommend him? Nothing. He was just like her father, a despicable charmer whose infidelities had caused her mother years of anguish. Even as a parent, Charles Harris had been unreliable, the pursuit of his numerous affaires often taking precedence over his paternal responsibilities. Though she hadn't discovered until later the reason why he broke promises to attend school plays and other functions.

Closing her mind to thoughts of past unhappiness, Liz washed Fielding's glass and put it away in a cupboard, as if removing the evidence of his presence would eradicate him from her thoughts. But, try as she might to concentrate on other matters, the impact of his personality, and the extra income he had offered her, continued to preoccupy her throughout her solitary evening meal.

It was the sort of wage that people paid for domestic and garden help in London, and no doubt he could well afford it. People who worked in television seemed to earn massive salaries. But was it right for her to accept it? It would certainly make a big difference to her somewhat straitened finances.

At eight o'clock, when Spanish telephone charges became cheaper than during the working day, she went up to the larger of the two small bedrooms which was now her workroom and where she used her computer.

After checking for incoming e-mails, her link with colleagues and friends now far away, she clicked on her Internet browser and went to a favourite website. The World Wide Web offered an escape from the problems of the real world. Sometimes she felt she might be becoming a Web addict, but at least it was a harmless addiction, not like taking to the bottle as some lonely widows did.

On Friday afternoon she rang his number.

'Cam Fielding.'

She would have recognised the distinctive timbre of his voice if he hadn't given his name. 'It's Liz Harris. If your offer is still open, I'd like to give it a try.'

'Splendid…that's excellent news. If you'll come round, I'll give you a set of keys and a quick tour of the house.'

'Now?'

'If it's convenient.'

When, five minutes later, he opened the door to her, he was wearing a coral linen shirt and pale khaki chinos.

Unlike her little house, his had a spacious hallway and a staircase with a beautiful wrought-iron balustrade that looked antique.

'Fiona is in the garden having a siesta,' he said, as he closed the door. 'We went to a nightclub on the coast. I hope our return in the small hours didn't disturb you.'

'A car wouldn't wake me,' she said. 'In the summer, when the nights were hot, the local dogs were a bit of a nuisance.'

He showed her around the ground floor. The windows on the street side were small, with protective iron *rejas*, but those on the south side had been replaced with tall windows with no *rejas* to obstruct the view of the mountains. There was a large kitchen with a big family-sized dining table at one end. Folding doors connected this to a living room lined with book-shelves and paintings. There was also a bedroom-cum-study lined with more books and, next to it, a spacious bathroom.

'This serves as the downstairs loo, and up-stairs there are more bedrooms and bathrooms,' he told her. 'Let me give you a cup of coffee and then we'll discuss the new arrangements.'

The daughter and wife of men with no domestic capabilities, Liz was always surprised by men who knew their way round a kitchen and could keep themselves fed and laundered with-out female assistance. Whether Fielding's competence extended beyond making coffee, she rather doubted. Though perhaps it might if his life as a roving reporter for a television news channel had, from what she had heard, taken him to many of the world's trouble spots where hotel facilities were not always available.

'I expect to be down here more often in the next twelve months,' he said, putting cups and saucers on a tray. 'How often, in your view, does the place need cleaning to keep it in reasonable order?'

Liz leaned on the rose marble worktop that divided the working part of the kitchen from the dining area. 'The kitchen and the bathrooms need more attention than the other rooms. I have no idea how efficiently Alicia cleans when she does clean. The most sensible plan might be for me to look in, say, every two weeks and suggest to her what needs doing.'

He gave her a smiling glance. 'I notice you say "suggest" not "tell". That sounds as if you have good management skills.'

Conscious of his charm, and resistant to it, she said, 'Most people prefer to be asked rather than ordered. That's just common-sense. For what you're prepared to pay me, I'm prepared to make sure that the house is always ready for occupation. Though, obviously, some notice of your arrival is important as far as stocking the fridge is concerned.'

'Give me your e-mail address and I'll give you mine,' he said. 'That way we can keep in touch easily. You'll find a notepad and pencils by the phone in the other room—' with a gesture towards the living room.

Liz fetched the pad and wrote her address for him. While waiting for the kettle to boil, he wrote down his for her. Then he spooned coffee powder from a jar of instant decaff into the cups, filled them with water and carried the tray to the table.

'I didn't buy Alicia's explanation of why the place was in a mess when we arrived,' he said. 'Hopefully, with you keeping an eye on her, she'll pull her socks up. If she doesn't, it may be necessary to find someone else. Perhaps you could make enquiries. I know a lot of the younger women have cars now and prefer to work in supermarkets and offices. But for the older women, without any transport, domestic work is still the only option.'

'I'll keep my ear to the ground,' said Liz. 'But it has to be said that cleaning an empty house for an absent employee is not much fun. Alicia may buck up a lot if you're going to be here more often, and if I'm around to applaud her efforts. Housework is horribly repetitive and women who do it need to feel appreciated.' She was thinking of her mother, whose excellent housekeeping had never been praised or even noticed.

He changed the subject. 'Do you mix with the other foreigners round here? Have they been friendly?'

'Very friendly...and so have the local people.' But, as she had already learned in England, there was a world of difference between the life of a wife and that of a widow. The social world was set up for pairs, not singles.

The door to the terrace opened and Fiona joined them. She was wearing the briefest possible silver two-piece swimsuit. As Fielding rose, she said, 'Is that coffee? Can I have some?' Only as an afterthought did she toss a 'hello' at Liz.

For something to say, Liz asked, 'Did you enjoy your night on the town?'

'It was OK.'

Fiona's indolent shrug made her breasts do a jelly-like wobble in their silver cups. Probably most men would find her nudity enormously sexy, Liz thought. But would a discriminating man? Wouldn't he think she was overplaying her seductiveness. Still, presumably sex, and lots of it, was the only reason she was here. She didn't give the impression of being a great conversationalist. She was not even good at the small talk that strangers tossed back and forth in situations like this.

Liz drained her cup. 'I'd better be off. I have a lot to do today.'

'Hang on a minute.' Fielding handed Fiona her coffee, then felt in his back packet and produced a billfold. 'You'd better have some money on account...both to pay Alicia and for yourself.'

'That really isn't necessary. We can settle up next time you're here.'

'Certainly it's necessary. I might get my head blown off by a terrorist and then where would you be?' He handed her some twenty *mil* bills. 'Tomorrow morning I'll call at the bank and arrange for the payments into your account to be altered. You also need the extra house keys I had cut. They're in a drawer in the hall.'

Following him from the kitchen, Liz said, 'Goodbye, Fiona.'

Fiona did say, 'Bye,' but she didn't bother to mask her indifference with a smile.

She must be fantastic in bed for him to put up with her abysmal manners, thought Liz, as she marched down the street, the money in her pocket, the keys to La Higuera in her hand.

When Cam returned to the kitchen, Fiona said, 'She ought to get that nose bobbed.'

'What's wrong with her nose?'

'It's too big.'

'So is mine,' he said, rubbing the prominent bridge inherited from his great-grandfather, Captain 'Hawk' Fielding. His features had been similar to those of the Afghan tribesmen against whom he had played the Great Game on the North West Frontier, eventually dying a hero's death in Kabul in the early years of Queen Victoria's reign. Cam had often thought it was probably a gene from his adventurous forebear that had dictated his own choice of career.

'That's different,' said Fiona. 'On a man a big nose is OK. On a woman it's not.'

'I only noticed her eyes. They're the colour of speedwells.' Realising that Fiona might never have seen a speedwell, he added, 'They're small wild flowers...the bluest of blues.'

'She doesn't like you,' said Fiona. 'Or me. She was looking down her big nose at both of us. But it didn't stop her taking your money.'

'Why do you think she doesn't like us?' Cam could guess why, but he doubted if Fiona could.

'I expect she envies you,' said Fiona. 'You're famous and rich and successful, and she's a nobody living in a grotty little house with no money. I shouldn't think she'll ever get another husband.'

'You're a luscious piece, but you don't have a kind heart, do you, Fifi?' he said dryly. 'My reading of Mrs Harris is that she likes her little house, she doesn't want to shop till she drops, and she's still in mourning.'

Fiona didn't like it when he called her Fifi. There were several things about him she didn't like. He could be sarcastic, and sometimes she had no idea what he was talking about. But she enjoyed being envied by other women who would like to be his girlfriend, and he didn't expect her to do all the work in bed, like some of the men she had known. In fact going to bed with him was a treat. She was in the mood for it now.

She gave him her most alluring smile. 'I'm going to have a shower. Care to join me?'

In the night, without waking Fiona, Cam got up and went downstairs for some water. In his twenties and early thirties he had got through a lot of alcohol, but nowadays he drank less and less, knowing what happened to journalists who went on hitting the booze into their forties.

He was fit, and he wanted to keep it that way. He had drunk more this week, with Fiona, than he had for a long time. And he knew why. Because she bored him. When they weren't actually in the sack, he found her a dull companion. It had been a mistake to bring her. This wasn't her kind of place. She liked shopping and smart restaurants and places to dance. It had been selfish of him to deprive her of the things she enjoyed. She was a playgirl, but he was no longer a playboy. It was time to recognise that fact, to restructure his life accordingly.

After drinking one glass of spring water, he carried another upstairs. The bedroom was full of moonlight. It illumined Fiona's unconscious face and the voluptuous curves outlined by the rumpled sheet.

Cam went to the window and looked out. Beyond the top of his garden wall was a row of Roman-tiled roofs, many tiles out of alignment, others speckled with lichen. Several of the houses were empty or used only for storage. There was only one flat roof, a conversion done by Beatrice Maybury.

Thinking about her successor, the buttoned-up Mrs Harris, he felt he had made a good move in appointing her to sort out his domestic problems. She seemed the conscientious type who would earn every peseta of the extra money he was paying her. She was certainly doing a much better job with the garden than Beatrice had.

At the same time he thought she was crazy to bury herself in a place like Valdecarrasca. Obviously, as he had said to Fiona, Liz Harris was still in mourning for her damned fool of a husband who had thrown away his life, and ruined hers, in a gallant act of madness. If his attempt had succeeded, he would have been a hero. Instead of which he was dead and she was condemned to a lonely future. He hadn't asked, but he felt sure there were no children. If there were, she wouldn't be here.

That she had accepted his offer, while privately disapproving of him, suggested that her work as a designer wasn't bringing in enough money. Not that she had shown her disapproval, but his job had made him an expert at picking up vibes. Like most 'good' women, she had a strict moral code that put free agents like himself and Fiona beyond the pale. Good women wanted everyone to live the way they did, the men in solid nine-to-five jobs like accountancy and the law.

But he had chosen a career that demanded he pack his bags at short notice and go to wherever the headlines were being made, usually somewhere bloody uncomfortable, from which there was always a chance he might not return. The casualty rate was high among war reporters and photographers. It wasn't a life to share with a wife and children. Some of his colleagues had tried, but usually it ended in divorce. It was wiser not to attempt it, or not until one retired. Which was what he was thinking of doing.

For almost twenty years he had run the gauntlet of violence in all the world's worst trouble spots and got through with only a graze from a bullet on his arm. His luck might not hold out much longer. Too many colleagues had died, or been badly injured, or resorted to dangerous forms of Dutch courage. It was time to call it a day and become a desk-bound presenter or, failing that, find some other way of earning his living.

He had a hunch the Internet held the key to his future and, if that hunch proved correct, he could live where he pleased, perhaps here in this peaceful village, so remote from the war zones where he had spent recent years that it might be on another planet.

Early one morning, a week after the *persianas* came down at La Higuera, Liz opened the Inbox on her e-mail program to find a message from Cameron Fielding. In the subject line, he had typed 'Congratulations on your website'.

Although the e-mail address she had written down for him was what was known as a dot com address, she was slightly surprised that he had bothered to check that the last part led to a website. But then she remembered he was a journalist, and curiosity was their stock in trade.

She read the main part of the e-mail he had written.

Dear Mrs Harris (or may I call you Liz?) I've been looking round your website. I'm impressed. Maybe you should switch from needlework designs to website design. I'm told there's a big demand for good site designers. How about making a start by designing a site for me? If you're willing to have a crack at it, I'll be happy to pay you the going rate.

Think it over.

Regards, Cam.

Liz printed out his e-mail and put it in her bag to re-read later. Today was the day she drove down to the coast to attend the weekly meeting of the Peñon Computer Club at Calpe.

According to elderly people who had known Spain before the tourist invasion, when she was a little girl Calpe had been a sleepy fishing village. Now it was a large resort with many tall blocks of apartments, most of them holiday flats or the year-round homes of retired expatriates.

Liz didn't like Calpe but acknowledged that lots of people did, and it took all sorts to make a world. She did enjoy the club meetings, although most of the other members were old enough to be her parents or even grandparents. But their shared enthusiasm for computers made the age difference unimportant. One or two of the old men were inclined to ogle her, and one was a furtive groper. But she could cope with that.

After the meeting, she and Deborah, a divorcee in her late forties who kept in touch with her children by e-mail, had lunch at a Chinese restaurant not far from the port. It was close to the Peñon de Ifach, a massive rock, a thousand feet high, that reared out of the sea and was a mecca for rock climbers from all over Europe.

'Have you ever walked up the path that goes up the other side of the Peñon?' she asked her friend.

Deborah shook her head. 'I don't have a good head for heights. Living on the higher floors of some of the apartment blocks would worry me!'

'Me too,' said Liz. 'I should feel uneasy sitting out on some of those tiny balconies. But a penthouse apartment with a garden might be nice. The views must be wonderful.'

After lunch she drove back to Valdecarrasca where, having no garage, she had to leave her seven-year-old vehicle in the car park near the building that had once been a *lavadero*, a public laundry with a stream running through it. Since then the stream had run dry and today, so Beatrice had told her, the water came from deep bore holes near a village at the far end of the valley. Nowadays everyone had mains water and washing machines but, in a country with little rainfall, the ever-increasing demand for water could not be met indefinitely.

After changing out of her good clothes into everyday things, she settled down to reply to Cameron Fielding's e-mail.

She didn't mind him calling her Liz, but she wasn't sure she wanted to call him Cam yet. However, to start 'Dear Mr Fielding' sounded rather stuffy in response to his informality, so she stretched a point and started off.

Dear Cam,
I'm glad you like my website and I'm flattered that you're willing to entrust the design of your site to me. As I have never done any designing for other people, I have no idea what the going rate is. But I can find out, and perhaps we can discuss the matter further next time you come down. I should have to ask you a lot of questions before I could create a site that satisfied us both. What would the purpose of the site be?
Liz.

After she had connected to the Spanish telephone company's freebie server, and sent the message on its way, she had a spasm of doubt about the wisdom of becoming any more involved with Cam Fielding than she was already.

From the first moment of meeting him, she had been on her guard with him. That being so, was it foolish to take on a commitment that, inevitably, would involve more contact with him? Would it have been more sensible to politely decline his suggestion on the grounds that she had more work than she could handle?

CHAPTER TWO

Entre col y col, lechuga

Variety is the spice of life

UNTIL Cam put the idea into her head, it had not struck Liz that there might be a better income to be made from designing websites than from her present occupation. A site commissioned by a 'name' as big as Cameron Fielding would certainly give such a venture a splendid start.

But would there also be a downside? Would designing a site for him involve a lot more personal contact than she wished for?

Cam's reply to her e-mail came into her Inbox the next time she logged on.

Liz,
In a couple of hours I'll be flying to the Middle East to cover the latest outbreak of hostilities. Hope to be back next week. Meanwhile I'll think about the kind of site I want. Maybe I'll be able to get down to V. for a night or two so that we can put our heads

together and get the basics sorted out.
Take care, Cam.

The phrase 'put our heads together' conjured
up a degree of intimacy that she wasn't comfortable with. At the same time she was increasingly curious to see him in his public persona.

Beatrice Maybury had not owned a television
set. She considered TV a waste of time. Liz had
had a set in England but had not brought it to
Spain, or bought a new set here. She preferred
reading anyway.

She was certainly not going to ask any of the
foreigners she knew if she could watch a news
programme on the channel Cam worked for.
That would immediately trigger more gossip on
the lines of—'Liz Harris has taken a shine to
the heart-throb at La Higuera, we hear. I wonder
how long it will take him to get her between the
sheets?' The thought of being the subject of lu-
bricious speculations made Liz cringe.

It was in the middle of another wakeful night
that she suddenly realised that his TV channel
would have a site on the Web where she might
find information about Cameron Fielding, foreign correspondent.

Although her computer was three years old,
and not equal to handling the very latest technology, she could pick up the ordinary stuff. She

sat up in bed and reached for the quilted dressing gown thrown over the footrail. The days
were still mild and warm, but at this time of year
there was a significant fall in the temperature
after sunset.

With her feet tucked into cosy slippers, she
went to her workroom and was soon online. It
took only moments to find the website she
wanted, and a few moments more to find a list
of the channel's presenters and reporters.

When she clicked on Cam's name, up came
a potted biography and a photograph. The sight
of his face looking out at her from the screen
had almost the same effect as when she had
scrambled to her feet in his garden and looked
into those amused grey eyes for the first time.

In an automatic reflex, she right-clicked with
the mouse, bringing up a menu that included the
option to save the picture to her hard drive.
Then, not wanting to, yet compelled to continue,
she saved the photograph in her My Documents
folder where it would remain until she chose to
delete it.

The bio at the side of the picture read:

*Cameron Fielding is arguably the best-
known of the élite group of internationally famous foreign correspondents who report
world news for television. He has been*

awarded the CBE *for his services to journalism.*

In a career spanning almost 20 years, Fielding has worked for the BBC, CNN, ITN *and* Sky News. *His reporting has won widespread critical acclaim and many awards including the* Amnesty International Press Award, *the* Reporter of the Year award *at the New York Festival of Radio and Television, the* James Cameron Award *for war reporting, and the* One World Broadcasting Trust Award. *He has also won the prestigious* Emmy Award *presented by the American National Academy of Television Arts & Sciences.*

Below this was a question-and-answer interview.

Q: Where did you grow up?
A: All over the place. My father's career involved frequent uprooting. My passport is British, but I was born in Hong Kong and spent my formative years in Tokyo, Rome, Madrid and Washington DC, so I count myself a citizen of the world.

Q: What was your first job?
A: I joined the BBC's World Affairs Unit after reading Modern History at university.

Q: What was the most memorable event you have reported?

A: I've covered a succession of memorable events: Tiananmen Square in 1989; Baghdad and the Gulf War 1991; famine in Somalia 1993; the Soweto riots 1996. Every year produces a major disaster. I wish the media would focus more on mankind's achievements. I think being swamped with bad news depresses people.

Q: What are your worst and best qualities?

A: Worst: I'm impatient, especially with petty bureaucracy. Best: Probably tolerance.

Q: If you could travel backwards in time, what era would you visit?

A: I'd like to have been the expedition reporter on Christopher Columbus's ship *Santa Maria* when, trying to reach the East by sailing westwards, he discovered the New World.

Q: What excites you and what depresses you?

A: I'm excited by the World Wide Web: I believe it has the potential to make life better for everyone. I'm depressed by self-satisfied, self-serving politicians.

As she re-read his answers to the questions, Liz was forced to admit that, had she known nothing about his personal life, the interview would have impressed her.

His childhood sounded far more exciting than hers. She had always longed to travel, but a possessive mother, shortage of money and falling in love with Duncan had conspired to prevent her from being anything but an armchair traveller. Now her wanderlust had diminished. From what she read, mass tourism and the popularity of back-packing had combined to make exotic destinations far less exotic than they had been when she was eighteen. The time to take off and see the world had been then, not now. As her grandmother had often said to her, 'Opportunity only knocks once'.

Liz shut down her computer and went back to bed. After she had switched out the light, for a while it was Granny she thought about. Granny had tried to dissuade her from marrying so young. 'You're not properly grown-up,' she had said. 'You've had no experience of life...or other men. There are more fish in the sea than Duncan.'

Knowing that her grandmother's marriage had not been happy, Liz had dismissed her advice.

But her last thought, before she slept, was not about Granny. In her mind's eye she saw the strong features of the man whose faced was filed on her computer.

Cam's e-mailed instruction, before his next visit, to have Alicia make up the bed in the room above the garage puzzled Liz until, on her own next visit to La Higuera, she went upstairs for the first time. It then became clear that the bedroom where she had seen him kissing Fiona was a comfortable guest room and the room over the garage was his room.

The first thing that caught her eye was a portrait on the wall between the two windows, obviously placed there so that the light wouldn't fade it. It was an oil painting of a man in the regimental dress uniform of a bygone age. He had an early Victorian hairstyle, but otherwise it might have been Cam in fancy dress. There was a small engraved brass plaque on the bottom of the ornate gilt frame. She had to go close to read the small writing—*Captain Nugent Fielding, 1st Bombay Light Infantry*. Clearly the captain was Cam's ancestor.

There were family photographs around the room and many other personal possessions. She found it interesting that he slept here when he was alone, but used a guest room when he had a girlfriend in residence. What would a psychologist make of that? she wondered. That he didn't want his private space invaded by any woman? That he saw women purely as sex objects and therefore, like kitchen equipment and garden tools, they belonged in certain areas, but not in here?

It was twelve-forty-five and she was about to wash the fruit she was having for lunch when the telephone rang.

'Hello?'

'It's Cam. I just got in. What are you doing for the next couple of hours?'

'Nothing in particular, but—'

'Then we'll go out to lunch. There's a lot to discuss. I'll pick you up in ten minutes, OK?'

Taking her consent for granted, he rang off.

Liz flew upstairs to her room, whipped off her house clothes and scrambled into grey gabardine trousers and a grey and white striped silk shirt. Slotting a belt through the loops on the waistband, she stepped into suede loafers, then put on her favourite gold knot earrings, hurriedly slapped on some make-up and re-brushed her hair before pulling it through a black scrunchy.

It was only when she was ready, with a couple of minutes to spare, that she asked herself, What am I doing, making an effort to look good for a man I don't even like?

There wasn't time to consider the answer to that question because, remembering that once summer was past the interior of Spanish restaurants could sometimes be chilly if they didn't have an open fire, she had to whizz back upstairs and grab her red shawl.

She was running downstairs when she heard a knock on the door. She had thought he would pip his car's horn to alert her to his arrival, but when she stepped into the street he was waiting to open the door for her. Quickly, Liz locked up and slid into the passenger seat. No doubt it was part of a womaniser's armoury to have impeccable manners, she thought as he bent to pull the safety belt out of its slot and handed her the buckle.

'Thank you.' She tried to recall a previous occasion when a man had performed that small extra courtesy but could not remember it ever happening before.

'So what's new in Valdecarrasca?' he asked, as he got in beside her and pulled the other belt across his own broad chest.

'Nothing…as far as I know. How did your trip go?'

'I've been dashing around the world, covering outbreaks of mayhem, for too long,' he said, checking his rearview and wing mirrors before pulling away from the kerb. 'It no longer gives me a buzz, which means it's time to call it a day and find something more rewarding to do.'

'What have you in mind?'

'It would be fun to do a Gerald Seymour.'

'The name rings a bell but I can't place him.'

'He used to be a war reporter. Now he writes excellent thrillers.'

'Oh, yes…I remember now. My husband used to like his books.' Not that Duncan had been a bookworm, but when they were going on holiday he would buy a thriller at the airport and often would still be reading it on the flight home.

'Unfortunately I don't think I have Seymour's imaginative powers,' said Cam, 'and, although there are exceptions, not many non-fiction writers make a comfortable living. By the way, the house is in the best shape it's been in since it was new. Your relationship with Alicia is obviously going well.'

'My Spanish is improving too,' said Liz. 'It's hard to get her to speak really slowly, but we're managing. I've started buying the Saturday edition of *El Mundo*. It has very good health and history supplements. It takes me all week to read them, but it's good for my Spanish vocabulary.'

'There are some Spanish novels on the shelves in the sitting room. If you want to borrow them, or any of the books, feel free,' Cam told her.

'That's very kind of you. If I do, I'll take good care of them.'

'If I had any doubts about that, I wouldn't have suggested it.' He took his eyes off the road for a moment to smile at her. 'I don't give many people the freedom of my library.'

The flattering implication that they were two of a kind, at least as far as books were concerned, was a small breach in her defences that she couldn't afford to let him repeat.

'If there are any wonderful restaurants around here, I haven't discovered them,' he went on. 'But Vista del Coll has a good view and the food is passable. Do you know it?'

'I've passed it. I haven't eaten there.'

'The clientele is an odd mix of elderly expats and Spanish workmen. At weekends and on *fiestas* it's packed with Spanish families. Young couples are reducing the number of children they have, but the different generations of the family still go out in a bunch in a way you don't often see in the UK,' he said. 'I like that.'

Liz made no comment. That she had no children, and probably never would have, was a sadness she had learned to live with. But sometimes, seeing other women with theirs, she felt an ache inside her.

It was only a short drive to the restaurant where, although it was early for lunch by Spanish standards, there were already several cars parked.

'Would you prefer to eat inside or outside?' Cam asked, as they mounted the steps to the terrace.

'It's such a lovely day, it seems a pity not to make the most of it.' Liz had left her shawl on the back seat of the car.

'That's my feeling too. How about there?' He indicated a table for four where they would both be able to sit facing the mountains.

Cam was drawing out a chair for her when the proprietor bustled out to greet them. Evidently he remembered Cam from previous visits and the two men—one short and rotund, the other tall and lean—had a conversation in rapid Spanish.

Then the other man gave a smiling bow to Liz and presented her with one of the two menus he was carrying.

'What about a drink while we're choosing what to eat?' Cam said. 'A glass of *vino blanco*, perhaps?'

'I'd rather have a glass of sparkling water.' She wanted to keep a clear head.

Cam's left eyebrow rose a fraction, but he didn't try to persuade her to change her mind.

The menu, she discovered, was set out in several languages. She read the Spanish page, keeping her finger in the English page in case there were dishes she could not translate.

With her bottle of spring water came a glass of white wine for Cam, a basket of crusty bread and a dish of *alioli* to spread on the bread.

'When I was in my teens, *alioli* was always made on the premises,' he told her. 'But then an increase in salmonella caused several bad cases of food-poisoning and restaurant hygiene regulations became a lot stricter. Now it's not home-made any more and doesn't have the same flavour.'

Liz sipped the refrigerated water and looked at the view. There was no denying that it was nicer being here, sitting in the sun with an interesting companion, than having lunch by herself at home.

'Were your father and grandfather journalists?' she asked, remembering what he had told her before, and what she had read about him online.

The question seemed to amuse him. 'Definitely not, and they didn't approve of my choice of career. They wanted me to follow them into the foreign service but fate decreed otherwise. Do you believe in fate?'

'I don't know. Do you?'

'No, actually I believe in chance. The chance that led me to break the family tradition happened in Addis Ababa...if you know where that is?'

'Of course...it's the capital of Ethiopia in north east Africa.'

'Your geography is above average. You'd be surprised by how many people I meet who have only the haziest idea where places are outside their own country. It happened during a vacation while I was at college. I was in Ethiopia when a munitions dump blew up, killing a TV reporter and leaving the cameraman and sound recordist without a front man. I persuaded them to let me stand in for the guy who was dead. I had beginner's luck. The reports we did were good enough to get me a place on the payroll as soon as I got my degree. How did you get your start?'

'As an office dogsbody. Then I worked up to being PA to the magazine's crafts editor. Needlework was my hobby. They were always short of good projects and they took some of my ideas. After a bit I was promoted to assistant crafts editor. I might, eventually, have succeeded her. But after... There came a point when I suddenly realised I hated the twice-daily commute and the whole big city thing. I'd had enough of northern winters and unreliable summers.'

'That's the way I feel. I'd like to spend nine or ten months of the year here, and the rest of the time networking in London, New York and wherever else I needed to keep up my contacts. That said—' He broke off as the proprietor came back, expecting to take their order.

When Cam explained they hadn't decided yet, he gave an accommodating shrug and turned away to greet some new arrivals.

'We had better make up our minds. What do you fancy?' said Cam.

'I'd like to start with a salad and then have the roast lamb, please.'

'You'll have some wine with the meal, won't you?'

Liz nodded. 'I like wine…but I can't knock it back like some of the expats I've met.'

'Oh, the drinks party crowd.' His tone was dismissive. 'You find them wherever there's a large foreign community. People who live abroad fall into two groups. One lot thrives in a different culture. The other never feels really comfortable. Have you met Valdecarrasca's first foreign residents, the Drydens?'

'I've heard them mentioned. I haven't met them. He's an American, isn't he?'

'Todd is one of those cosmopolitan Americans who has spent more time outside the US than in it. He used to be something important in the oil business and then, in his forties, he had a heart attack and nearly didn't make it. They decided to downsize their lives and came to Spain, where Leonora discovered she had a genius for doing up derelict *fincas* and transforming them into desirable residences for well-heeled rain exiles.'

'They live in that house near the church with cascades of blue morning glory and purple bougainvillaea hanging over the wall, I believe?'

'That's right. Leonora bought it years ago, when they were living on the coast near where Todd's yacht was berthed. She bought up a lot of properties. Prices were much lower then. The hinterland was unfashionable. I expect you'll be asked to the Drydens' Christmas party. It's when they give newcomers the once-over. Those who pass muster are invited again. Those who don't, aren't. Leonora doesn't suffer fools and bores gladly.'

'She sounds rather daunting,' said Liz.

'She's a doer,' said Cam. 'She has no patience with people who aren't. She'll be impressed by your courage in coming here on your own.'

'It wasn't courage. It was desperation,' she said lightly. 'I was in a rut and I had to get out of it.'

Cam signalled to the proprietor, who came back and took his order. When he asked, '...*y para beber?*' Cam turned to her.

'Would you like red or white wine? Or they have a good *rosado*, if you prefer it?'

'I'm easy,' she said, without thinking, and then wished she hadn't. Not that he was likely to read the alternative meaning into her answer. Or was he?

The order completed, Cam picked up her remark about being in a rut. 'I feel much the same. I don't know if there's any scientific basis for the idea that our bodies go through seven-year cycles of change, but I think it's a good idea to review one's life every ten years or so. I don't want to spend my forties the same way I spent my thirties and twenties. It's been a lot of fun, but now it's time for something new.'

The wine arrived. Here, Liz noticed, the usual restaurant ritual of pouring a little into the host's glass and waiting for his approval was ignored. It was taken for granted the wine would be drinkable. This would have disappointed Duncan and her father-in-law, who had both enjoyed the pretence of being connoisseurs. It didn't seem to bother Cam.

When both their glasses had been filled, he thanked the young waiter and said to her,

'Here's to us…an escapee from the rat-race and a would-be escapee.'

Liz responded with a polite smile, not entirely comfortable with a link that seemed tenuous, to say the least.

She was even less comfortable when, after they had both tasted the wine, he proposed a second toast. 'And to your new venture as a website designer…with me as your first client.'

She put her glass on the table. 'I think we need to discuss that before we drink to it. That's why we're here…to talk business,' she reminded him.

'Certainly, but business goes better when it's combined with pleasure, don't you think? For me, it's much more enjoyable having lunch with an attractive, elegant woman than with a teenage or twenty-something techie who knows all the IT answers but not much else.'

Liz decided it was time to put her cards firmly on the table. 'As long as it's clearly established that business is where it begins and ends. You have the reputation of being a—' she searched for the politest term for it '—an habitual ladies' man and, in the last four years, I've found that a lot of men think a widow is a sitting target. I just want to make it clear that I'm not.'

As soon as she had made this statement, she felt she had gone too far and the lunch, far from being enjoyable, would be ruined by deep umbrage on his side and acute embarrassment on hers.

'I'm sorry if that sounded rude. It wasn't intended to. I only want to avoid any... misunderstanding. It's not that I have an inflated idea of my attractiveness. I don't. Compared with Fiona Lincoln...' She felt she had said enough and left it at that.

While she was speaking, Cam had leaned back in his chair, watching her with an expression she could not interpret. Now the flicker of a smile appeared at the corners of his mouth.

'It must be very annoying to have passes made that you haven't encouraged,' he said mildly. 'You'll be relieved to hear that I never do that. I only make passes at women who indicate, beyond doubt, that they would welcome a closer relationship—and not always then,' he added dryly. 'So now you can relax, *señora*. If I tell you I like your clothes, it will be a straightforward comment like saying that I like the shapes of those mountains—' with a gesture at the craggy crests to the south of the valley.

At this point, to her relief, their first course arrived. Liz's salad was more imaginative than the standard Spanish restaurant salad that often consisted of lettuce, tomato, onion and a few olives. Here, the chef had added hard-boiled egg, grated carrot, sweetcorn and pickled red cabbage, the last perhaps a concession to the taste of German patrons.

Cam had chosen *canelones* and they came in a small round glazed clay dish, hot from the oven or, more likely, the *microonda.*

A combination bottle containing oil in one section and wine vinegar in the other was on his side of the table, its surface covered by a white paper cloth anchored to the undercloth by plastic clips. Cam passed the bottle to her, and the pepper and salt.

'Thank you.' Liz loved olive oil, especially the green-gold first pressing that was not always provided in restaurants, although it was in this one.

Cam said, 'When my grandparents came to Spain it was easy to get cooks and maids. They had a wonderful cook called Victoria who didn't only cook the specialities of this region but dishes from the other provinces. Spain is intensely provincial and they all think their ways are the best.'

He spoke as if nothing had happened to disturb the ease of their conversation. He broke off a piece of bread and dipped it into the red sauce covering the three stuffed rolls of pasta that were his starter. Putting the bread in his mouth, he chewed for a moment, then gave a satisfied nod. 'This isn't out of a bottle. Now…to business. You asked, in an e-mail, about the purpose of my website. I suppose what I want is a CV, but also something more than that…' He began to elaborate.

Their discussion of his requirements went on through the rest of the meal, only occasionally interrupted by remarks on other topics.

He had also chosen lamb for his main course and, when it was served, Liz said, 'One of the things I love about living here is going up to my roof and seeing a shepherd and his flock and his dogs passing somewhere near the village.'

'Have you noticed how they lead their flocks, not drive them? As a boy, I knew a shepherd. He was a gentle sort of guy who hated having to take his sheep to the *matadero*, the slaughter-house.'

'At least they enjoy their lives while they are alive,' said Liz. 'It bothers me when animals are kept in unnatural conditions. Do you eat out a lot when you're here? I'm sure Alicia would cook for you, if you wanted it.'

'I can cook, if I need to. Victoria taught me how to make a *caldo* and a *tortilla*. Sometimes foreign correspondents find themselves stuck in situations where they need practical skills as well as the gift of the gab.'

He topped up her glass, making Liz suddenly aware that the bottle was three-quarters empty and he hadn't had the lion's share. She had drunk more than she'd intended and must be careful to make this glassful last. She had never had enough to make her tight and wasn't sure what her limit was.

'I don't do puddings,' said Cam, when their plates were being removed. 'But don't let that put you off. The *flan* here is home-made, not served in a plastic pot.'

'I don't do puddings either. Too many calories. Why don't you eat them?'

'I'm a cheese man, and generally speaking the cheeses of Spain aren't wonderful. *Cabrales*, a goat's cheese wrapped in leaves, is good, but it's rare to find it in restaurants and you don't see it often in supermarkets.' His glance took in as much of her figure as he could see. 'You don't look as if you have a weight problem.'

'I don't, but I think I might if I didn't watch it. I walk on the lanes through the vineyards every day, but that, and a bit of gardening, is not a great deal of exercise. Most of the time, I'm sitting.'

'Talking of the garden, let's go back and have our coffee there. I have some ideas for improving it that I'd like your opinion on.' He signalled for the bill.

In the light of his assurance that he never made passes without encouragement, and assuming he was a man of his word, Liz had no grounds for feeling uneasy about going back to his place for coffee in the middle of the day. It would have been different at night, but then it was most unlikely they would ever have dinner together. Nevertheless she did feel slightly uneasy. Mainly, perhaps, because he was agreeable company and she didn't trust herself to remain impervious to his charm if they were together too often.

When they reached his house, he said, 'Sit tight while I open the garage.'

He unlocked the metal up-and-over door and swung it open. Earlier, watching him eat, she had wondered how he kept fit. Inside the garage, she saw a mountain bike and a shelf bearing several pairs of heavy walking boots.

Before he closed the outer door of the garage, Cam unlocked the door to the terrace for her. She did not offer to help with the coffee but left him to deal with it while she went down to the steps to the garden and settled herself on one of the two park benches with metal arms and wooden seats. The bench at the west end of the garden was close to two huge lavender bushes that were in flower with a score of bees working on them.

She had sometimes sat on this bench for a few minutes at the end of her gardening sessions. She wondered what changes he wanted to make, and then her thoughts drifted back to the garden of the suburban semi-detached where she and Duncan had lived together for thirteen years, slightly more than a third of her lifetime.

Cam came down the steps carrying a folding table that he set up in front of the bench. Soon afterwards he reappeared with a tray. As well as the coffee things there were two liqueur glasses and a bottle on it. Liz's doubts about his intentions reactivated.

'I mustn't stay long. What are your ideas for the garden?' she asked.

Instead of answering the question, he said, 'What's your hurry? Why not relax for the rest of the afternoon?' He checked the stainless steel watch that circled his muscular wrist. 'It's past three o'clock now.'

'I want to type out the things we discussed about your website while they're still clear in my head.'

'I can save you the trouble. I'll send you a copy of my notes. Is it OK to send them as an attachment, or do you regard e-mail attachments in the same light as unprotected sex?'

She knew then that he thought her a prude, and perhaps she was, because, coming from him, even a joking reference to sex made her uneasy.

Forcing herself to sound composed, she said, 'I certainly wouldn't open an attachment sent by a stranger, or with come-ons like ''Free'' or ''Win a million dollars'' in the subject line. But I'm sure your computer is effectively virus-protected.'

'It's protected. How effectively I'm not sure. The hackers seem to invent new viruses faster than the anti-virus guys can pile up the barricades.'

While they were talking he had been pouring the coffee. After placing a cup in front of her, he put a glass alongside it and reached for the bottle.

'Not for me, thank you,' said Liz.

'You don't like liqueurs...or you don't like *poire William*.'

'I've never tried it, but I think any more alcohol might give me a headache.'

'You've only had three glasses of wine. That's not heavy drinking, especially with meat and two veg. Come on, let me give you a small one.'

'I don't want it, Cam. Please don't press me.'

'I shouldn't dream of pressing you to do *anything* you didn't want to.' He took the glass away from her cup and placed it next to his own, pouring a generous measure of the liqueur for himself. 'But your nervousness does make me wonder what you've been told about me. Am I accused of luring respectable women into my garden and plying them with potent liqueurs before attempting to have my wicked way with them?'

Liz grabbed the strap of the shoulder bag she had hung on the back of the bench. Jumping up, she said crossly, 'If you're going to take that tack, I'm going home…now.'

She was halfway to the steps when he hooked his hand in the bend of her elbow and stopped her. As, angrily, she swung to face him, he said, 'You're making a fuss about nothing. I was only teasing you.'

'I'm not amused,' she said hotly.

And then, as they faced each other, her indignation evaporated, replaced by a different and unfamiliar emotion.

For a long, tense moment they looked at each other and she saw his expression change from a smile to a look she could not define or describe.

All she knew was that, for several seconds, some kind of current was switched on and flowed between them.

Then he released her arm and said quietly, 'Come back and drink your coffee and let's talk about the garden.'

Dazed and disturbed by what she had just experienced, Liz returned to the bench and sat down. As if nothing had happened, Cam began to outline his ideas. Forcing herself to concentrate, she listened to him.

'The last time I was here, I went to a party in a garden where the owners had made clever use of a large piece of mirror glass. They'd placed it so that it appeared to be an ivy-clad archway leading to another garden. Do you think we could copy that here?'

Liz drank some coffee and thought about the suggestion. 'You would have to try it out with a small piece of mirror. I go to the *rastro* at Benimoro most Saturdays. I could probably pick up a mirror for a few hundred pesetas.'

'Could you? That would be great.' He explained his other ideas, one of which involved getting a local builder to construct a walled bed for shrubs against the side of the terrace.

Eventually the conversation came to a natural end and when Liz got up to go he did not attempt to detain her.

She left by way of the house in order for Cam to give her a *Time* magazine he had bought for his flight down and thought she might like to read.

She had turned the corner into the short length of downhill street that connected his street and her street when she encountered a middle-aged woman she knew by sight who was holding a baby in one of the quilted bags in which recently born infants were often carried about.

By now Liz knew that baby girls could be recognised by the earrings they wore from soon after birth. The appropriate comment was an admiring, *'Qué guapa!'* if the child was female or, in the absence of earrings, the masculine form of the word meaning pretty or handsome.

Often the babies were beautiful only to their parents and grandparents, but this tiny boy was a charmer with large dark eyes and a mop of quite thick black hair. As Liz touched his petal-soft cheek with a gentle finger, a wave of sadness washed over her.

She controlled her feelings until she was safely indoors, but then the repressed emotion welled up again and she found herself in tears. It was most unlike her to cry. Perhaps it was partly reaction to the stresses of lunching with Cam. But mostly it was the reminder that in a few years it would be too late for her to have a baby of her own.

She had wanted to start a family two years after her marriage, though Duncan had been less keen. When she was twenty-five, after tests, her doctor had assured her there was no medical reason for her failure to conceive. At his suggestion, Duncan had undergone tests. The results had shown that the only way they could have children was by adoption, which her husband had not wished to do.

She was drying her eyes and pulling herself together when there was a knock on the door. She expected the caller to be the woman across the street who, if the postman left a package on Liz's doorstep while she was out, would take charge of it till she returned. But when she opened the door, it was Cam who stood outside.

'You forgot your shawl,' he said, handing it to her.

'Oh…thank you. I'm sorry you had the bother of bringing it down. Thank you very much.' Was her mascara smudged? Would he see she had been crying? Flustered, she closed the door.

Cam walked back to La Higuera wondering what had made her cry. She didn't seem the weepy type. He felt sure it had nothing to do with her angry flare-up in the garden. It would take more than that to reduce her to tears. Anyway, by the time she left that had been smoothed over.

He remembered that when, during lunch, he had asked her about her working life in England, she had spoken of the probability that she would have succeeded the crafts editor. She had started to say 'But after...' and then paused and begun again with 'There came a point when I suddenly realised...'

'But after my husband died...' was probably what she had intended to say but had changed her mind. Suggesting that, even after four years, remembering him still upset her.

Cam had never been in love, and in his world marriages seldom lasted. But he had not forgotten how lost his grandfather had been after his grandmother's death. He had enough imagination to guess what a devastating blow to Liz her husband's death must have been.

She was too young and attractive to live alone and, despite her making it clear that she wasn't in the market for an affair, should he have had that in mind, her body was ready for sex even if her mind rejected the idea of making love with anyone but her late husband.

The proof of that was in the way she had reacted when he stopped her walking out on him.

'I'm not amused,' she had stormed at him, and then something had sparked between them that he had recognised as mutual desire. Whether she had known what it was he was inclined to doubt. In four years of living as chastely as a nun, her senses atrophied by grief, she might have forgotten the buzz of physical attraction.

One of the Ancient Greek philosophers—probably Aristotle—had said that human beings had three basic motivations: hunger, thirst and lust. Liz was the kind of woman who would repudiate lust unless love was involved.

The idea that she could want a man whom she didn't trust would be repugnant to her. But for a moment or two she *had* wanted him, and he her. Not that he was going to do anything about it. You couldn't mix business with pleasure, and Liz was too much of an asset in her triple roles as gardener, Alicia's supervisor and the designer of his website for him to risk having a more personal relationship with her. Not that he wouldn't enjoy bringing her back to life and making her glow again. He could visualise how lovely she would be with her blue eyes sparkling with vitality instead of shadowed by unhappiness. But, at least for the time being, it was more important to establish a friendship, getting her to the point where she could take his teasing without getting uptight.

The day after Cam left, Liz went for her usual walk through the vineyards. Though the sky was blue, the air was cooler and the outlines of the

surrounding mountains were more sharply de-
fined than in warmer weather. Though in certain
lights they seemed to merge with each other,
there were seventeen mountains visible from the
village. She was beginning to know them by
name and keep their shapes in her mind's eye.

Her own house could not be seen from where
she was walking, but La Higuera stood out
from the smaller houses around it. When the
persianas were down, the windows looked like
closed eyes. She wondered how long it would
be before Cam came again, and if he would
keep in touch by e-mail or, now that she knew
what sort of website he wanted, he would leave
it to her to contact him.

She had not seen him again after he had
brought her shawl back. He had said goodbye
by means of a brief e-mail. By the time she read
it, he was already on his way to Valencia airport.

The strange feeling she had experienced in his
garden, while he had hold of her arm, continued
to fidget her. She had never felt anything like it
before, except occasionally when a passage in a
book or a scene in a movie had started a quiver
of excitement deep inside her.

But it had been anger she felt towards Cam,
and how could anger change to that deep puls-
ing excitement in a matter of seconds?

She did not like the feeling that, however briefly, she had lost control of the situation and might not have resisted if he had chosen to…

Closing her mind to the thought of what might have happened, she promised herself she would make sure that all their future encounters were kept on a strictly business footing.

CHAPTER THREE

En la batalla de amor, el que huye es el vencedor

In the battle of love, he who flees is the winner

BY THE time Cam came back, a month later, the valley had changed.

Two days of strong west winds had blown away most of the vine leaves. Some of the old vines had been grubbed up and the reddish clay soil rotavated. Shepherd's purse was springing up in the spaces between the vines, attracting flocks of noisy little finches. There were also some white egrets flying about, Liz had noticed on her daily walks.

Notifying her of his arrival twenty-four hours beforehand, Cam had added a postscript—'I've had what I hope is a brainwave. Looking forward to talking it over with you.'

In his absence she had made good progress with the design and coding of his website. But whether it would come up to his expectations remained to be seen. She could have sent the documents for him to view on his Internet browser, but she wanted to see his facial reactions the first time he looked at them.

On the evening he was due to arrive, Liz went to the eight p.m. showing of an English language film at the cinema at Gata de Gorgos, a town nearer to the coast.

She liked going to a movie occasionally but, more importantly, she wanted to be out in case he rang up and suggested they dine together to discuss his brainwave. Rather than make excuses, which he might overrule, it was easier not to be at home.

Although she knew that, in Spain's big cities, people dined as late as ten o'clock and the streets were still busy at midnight, this was not the norm in Valdecarrasca. When, coming home, she drove through the village, the square was deserted and all the houses in the main street had their shutters closed or their blinds down.

While the kettle was boiling for a cup of tea, she checked for e-mails. There was a message from Cam. 'If you're free tomorrow morning, could you come round at ten?'

Liz typed a one-word answer. 'Yes.'

As she logged off and closed down her PC, she was reluctantly aware that tomorrow was going to be a more exciting day than any since his last visit. It annoyed her that this should be so, but she couldn't deny it.

Next morning she washed her hair two days sooner than was strictly necessary. After breakfasting in her dressing gown and, aided by a dictionary, reading a page of a Spanish novel she had found on Cam's shelves, she went upstairs to dress. What to wear? Jeans and a sweatshirt? Or the kind of outfit she had worn to work in her previous life?

After looking through her wardrobe, she compromised between rustic casualness and city smartness by selecting the same gabardine trousers she had worn to lunch with him and a plain dark blue cashmere sweater bought in a sale. As a finishing touch she knotted a blue and grey kerchief round her neck with the ends above her left shoulder.

'Hello…good morning,' said Cam, as he opened the door.

The double greeting was one she had learnt to use with the Spaniards she met on her walks. But most of them were elderly men who might have exuded *machismo*, as he did, when they were younger but had long since lost it apart for a vestigial sparkle in the eye when she smiled at them.

'Good morning,' she said, rather formally, as she entered the hall.

'Coffee's on.' He gestured for her to precede him into the kitchen. 'Thank you for stocking the fridge. Here's what I owe you.' He indicated some banknotes placed on the kitchen counter where she had left the receipt from the supermarket.

'Thank you.' Seeing at a glance that the notes amounted to more than she had spent, Liz took her wallet from her bag. 'I'll give you your change.'

'No change is necessary,' he said. 'You forgot to charge for your petrol and your time.'

'I shouldn't dream of charging you for either,' she said firmly, putting down the change before she picked up his notes. 'I have to go shopping for myself. It's no trouble to pick up a few things for you occasionally.'

Cam gave her a thoughtful look. 'OK, if you insist. But what did that large piece of mirror glass you've found for me cost?'

'It was only a *mil*, but if it's not what you want I can take it back.'

'It's exactly what I want, and where you've positioned it is perfect.' He handed her a thousand-peseta note. 'It must have been an awkward thing to transport and put in place...or did you have help?'

'My car has a hatchback so it wasn't a problem getting it here. The man down the road,

Roberto, saw me getting it out of the car and offered to help. I wondered if I ought to give him the price of a drink, but then I thought it was better not to risk offending him.'

'I'll buy him a drink and thank him next time I go to the bar,' said Cam.

'Which bar do you go to?' she asked, surprised that he went to either. The village bars were fairly rough-and-ready establishments with fruit machines and a TV permanently on, not the sort of places he was used to.

'I have a drink in both of them occasionally. The noise level is hard on the eardrums, but the gossip can be amusing. Most foreigners aren't aware of it, but the village is a hotbed of politicking and rivalries.'

'It must be great to be fluent in Valenciano as well as Spanish. I don't think I'm ever likely to achieve that. Even if I did, the women don't seem to use the bars. The older ones get together in small sewing-bees outside each other's houses.'

'Do you miss the company of women of your own age?' he asked, making the coffee.

'No, not at all. There are lots of special interest organisations run by and for the expat community. I could go to a different meeting every day, if I wanted. But the Peñon Computer Club is the only thing I've joined. I'm not like someone who has retired. I don't have hours of spare time to fill.'

'No, but we all need congenial company. Is the computer club fun?'

'It's very male-orientated,' she said, before it occurred to her that this might be a contentious comment to make to someone as manifestly masculine as Cam.

'In what way?' he asked.

'Men have an affinity with machines that I don't think most women do. The guys at the club love tinkering with their computers' innards. I would rather not know about what goes on inside the systems unit. I just want it to run as smoothly as the washing machine or the fridge. If something *does* go wrong, I want to be able to call an engineer to fix it, not have to do it myself.'

'I should have thought the guys at the club would be falling over themselves to come and fix it for you. Or are they the ones who have made unwelcome passes?' he asked.

'I haven't had any serious computer problems since I've been here. If I did, I wouldn't expect someone who lives on the coast to come trailing out here to help.'

'There must be youths in the village who could sort out any but the most complex problems for you. Ask Alicia if she knows any teenage computer buffs. There are bound to be some around.'

'I'm sure there are, but the language barrier would be even worse with technical matters.'

'Not necessarily. Like cars, computers work in much the same way the world over. Shall we have our coffee on the terrace?'

When they went outside, she found he had put out two director's chairs, a dark green sunbrella and a camp stool to support the tray.

'I expect you like to sit in the shade. After last week's weather in London, I can't get enough of the sun,' said Cam. 'Do you mind if I take my shirt off?'

'Of course not.' Liz was beginning to wonder if, even sitting in the shade, she was going to be too hot in her sweater. The temperature inside her house was many degrees lower than on his sun-baked terrace. She should have put on a shirt.

Cam was unbuttoning his. She focused her gaze on the mountains to the south, and said, 'I'm very keen to hear about your brainwave. Do I gather it has to do with your website?'

'It will, if you think it's workable. But you may not.'

'Tell me about it.'

Without looking, she was aware that he was tugging his shirt free from his shorts. She had already taken in that his long legs were tanned, suggesting that, even if he hadn't been in Spain much this year, he had spent time in the sun elsewhere.

'I got the idea from a television advertisement that ran for a while last year, or maybe the year before,' he said. 'You may have seen it. I can't remember the product it was advertising, but it was a spoof dinner party and the guests included Marilyn Monroe, Albert Einstein and other celebrities whose names I've forgotten.'

'I didn't see it,' said Liz. 'But I did see an advertisement for a car which showed Steve McQueen apparently driving it years after he had died. Rather spooky, I thought...technology being able to resuscitate someone like that.'

'It is spooky,' Cam agreed, 'but also very clever. My idea has nothing to do with reviving the famous. What I have in mind is simply to interview six or eight interesting people about a particular subject and present the results as table-talk written in hypertext—that is with illustrations and links and perhaps sound clips. The overall title would be ''Cam Fielding's Dinner Parties'', each with a subtitle indicating the subject.'

'I think it's a terrific idea,' Liz said eagerly. 'Not complicated to do, and a wonderful draw

to your site. Have you started making guest lists
and choosing subjects?'

'Not yet. I wanted to see if you thought it was
workable. I did do a quick Web-search to check
if anyone else was already using the idea, but
all I came up with was recipes and tips for holding real-world dinner parties.'

'I was going to suggest a search,' said Liz.
'If someone else was already doing it, that might
have been a snag. Otherwise it sounds perfectly
workable. My only concern is that you might do
better to find an experienced professional designer to handle it for you, rather than an ama-
teur like me.'

She was looking at him as she spoke. She
couldn't fail to be aware that he was now
stripped to the waist and she was within touching distance of the most beautiful male torso she
had ever seen. His shoulders and chest must
delight any sculptor in search of a subject epit-
omising strength and grace. His body was as far
removed from beefcake as truly beautiful girls
were in a class apart from the silicone-breasted
bimbos of the soft porn magazines. She was
gripped by a crazy and quickly controlled impulse to reach out and stroke the smooth brown
skin covering the muscles cladding the perfectly
proportioned bone structure.

'My feeling is that most of the so-called professionals in this relatively new area of mass communication are far too keen on flashy gimmicks,' said Cam. 'Did you bring your design ideas with you?'

'Yes.'

'Right...when we've finished our coffee you can give me a demo on my laptop. I do use it out of doors sometimes, but in this case it's probably better to go inside.'

Ten minutes later, with the laptop set up on the big table in the kitchen, two chairs placed side by side and the *persiana* lowered so that sunlight would not fall on the screen, everything was in readiness for Liz to display her work to him.

She was accustomed to using a mouse, but Cam's laptop had a touchpad and, although she had tried one out at the computer club, she was not as adept as she would have liked to be. Also, although he had replaced his shirt when they moved indoors he had not bothered to button it and she was still disturbingly aware of his body.

She inserted the floppy disk, on which the documents that made up her design for him were stored, into the disk drive and, less expertly than she would have done with a mouse, transferred the folder she had named 'Fielding' to the laptop's hard drive where it would display faster.

She was seated on Cam's left with the edges of their chairs almost touching and their thighs parallel under the table. Before bringing up the opening screen, she said, 'As you'll see in a moment, I've designed areas that, if you like them and want to keep them, will need specially written text. For the time being I've put in place-holders. There you go...' This as she opened the website's homepage for him.

She had expected that he would move the laptop so that it was directly in front of him rather than, as at present, in front of her. Instead he rested his left arm along the back of her chair and, leaning closer to her, began to study the design.

Knowing that she wouldn't be comfortable staying like this for the ten minutes or longer that it might take him to navigate around the entire layout, Liz said, 'If it's all right with you, I'll make some more coffee.'

'Sure...go ahead.' As she rose, he gave her a glance that made her wonder if he suspected her real reason for moving.

From a more comfortable distance, by the worktop where the kettle was plugged in, she watched him become engrossed in what he was seeing on the screen.

What he was thinking as he inspected each section was impossible to tell. As the minutes passed, she found her insides beginning to knot with tension. So much depended on whether he liked it. If he did, it could be the beginning of a whole new phase of her life. If he didn't, many hours' work would have been wasted. Well, no, not totally wasted, she corrected herself, because she had enjoyed doing it. But the chances of her being able to sell her skills to anyone else of his stature were small.

The kettle boiled and Liz made two more cups of coffee, adding to his the amount of milk she had noticed he liked. She carried his cup and saucer to the table. Without glancing up, he said, 'Thanks.'

To her surprise, she saw that what he was looking at was the normally invisible code that most Web-surfers never saw and many didn't know existed.

'I see you've even spent time putting in meta tags,' he said.

'Because I think they're so important. Again they are only place-holders. You'll want to improve on them.'

Cam closed the screen showing the code and leaned back in his chair. 'I don't think they can be improved. The whole thing is brilliant...far better than I expected, to be honest, and way beyond anything I had visualised myself.'

Relieved and delighted by his praise, Liz reacted by saying, 'Really?'

'Yes, really. So what's the next step? Where do we go from here?'

Up to now she had not allowed herself to think beyond his reaction to the basic design.

'I guess the first thing to do is to register your dot com address, and then to decide who you want to host the site.'

'Can you handle the registration for me?'

'If you'll trust me with one of your credit card numbers.'

Cam frowned. 'Hmm…I'm not sure about that.'

For a disconcerting moment she thought he was serious. Then his cheeks creased in that dangerously charming smile that did things to her pulse-rate. 'I would trust you with *all* my card numbers. The world is full of con artists, but I don't think you're one of them. I'll write it down for you.' He rose from the table to use the notepad by the telephone. 'Here you are. Now, tell me who hosts your website.'

Liz told him, explaining the reasons for her choice.

She had noticed before that when Cam listened he gave his full attention to the person talking.

At the end of her explanation, he said, 'If they're good enough for you, they're good enough for me. Can I leave that to you as well?'

'By all means.'

'In that case the only thing left to settle is what I'm going to pay you. I've been looking into that and, frankly, I consider some of the fees being asked are lunatic. I suspect that a lot of people who haven't a tenth of your skills are trying to make some fast bucks from people to whom the Net is unknown territory.'

He then proposed a monthly retainer that was twice what she had expected he might be willing to pay her.

'In view of the experimental nature of this venture for both of us, I think we should try it for six months and see how it works out. At the end of that time we'll be in a better position to frame a more formal agreement. In the meantime, are you happy to go ahead on an informal basis?'

'Yes, perfectly happy. I think you're being generous. I'll do my best to merit your confidence in me.'

'Then let's shake on it.' He offered his hand.

The firm grip of his long strong fingers, and the effect that the physical contact had on her, reminded Liz that she was sealing an agreement with a man who, although he had brought her an unexpected opportunity to increase her income and break new ground professionally, was still someone whose values and standards were far removed from her own.

For the next hour they discussed the website in detail, both making notes. She had the satisfying feeling that, on this level, they could work well together.

She almost forgot about the personal level until, as the church clock began to strike twelve, he said, 'I think we should celebrate our partnership properly. How about dinner tonight?'

Immediately Liz's alarm system went into red alert mode.

'I'm afraid I'm going out tonight,' she said untruthfully.

'Are you free on Thursday?'

'Thursday is my Spanish conversation class.' The class started at six and finished at seven but she saw no need to tell him that. In case he intended to ask if she were free on Friday, she said hurriedly, 'I think to celebrate now would be premature. Wouldn't it be better to wait until the website is online?'

'Perhaps you're right. That's a date, then. When the site is launched, we'll party.'

There was something in the way he said it that made her suspect he knew she was being elusive and it brought out the predator in him.

The church clock began to strike noon for the second time. 'Why does it do that?' she asked him, relieved to turn the conversation in a safer direction.

'I don't know. I must ask.'

'Perhaps Alicia would know,' Liz said, preparing to leave. 'Though she isn't much help with plant names. I asked her about the climber with the yellow flowers growing up the wall by your log store. It grows all over the place, but she doesn't know its name.'

Cam surprised her by saying, 'Its botanical name is *Senecio angulatus*. It comes from South Africa, I was told by a friend who's a botanist. How it came to Spain, who can say? I'll walk to the corner with you. I need to go to the bank.'

They parted at the end of the street where he turned in the direction of the grandly named Plaza Mayor and she in the direction of her house. Walking the short distance to her front door, Liz wondered if she had been stupid to wriggle out of having dinner with him. After all, he had assured her that he didn't make passes without encouragement. More to the point, why should he feel impelled to come on strong with a woman in her late thirties, who had never been more than averagely presentable, when there were luscious creatures like Fiona willing to go to bed with him?

During the evening Cam rang Liz's number. If she answered, he intended to apologise, in Spanish, for dialling the wrong number. However, as he'd expected, the number was engaged. She was at home, not out as she'd said she would be. Of course there was the possibility that whoever she had been going out with had been forced to call it off at the last moment. He thought it a lot more likely that Liz had been telling a lie to avoid having dinner with him.

There could be two reasons for that: she didn't like him, or she didn't believe his promise not to pounce on her. Cam did not expect the entire female sex to like him, but experience told him that this attraction was mutual. So why was Liz unwilling even to have dinner with him?

Could it be that, still grieving for her husband, she felt that even to have dinner with another man was a kind of infidelity?

For her own sake, she needed to be shown that grief, however profound, was an unnatural state for someone of her age. She was too young to live on memories of past happiness. It was time to put the past behind her. Why had she come to Spain if not to start a new life?

After heating up one of the ready-made pizzas she had put in his fridge, he booted up his laptop and took another look at the website she had designed for him. There was something almost uncanny about the way she had realised all his own half-formed ideas about how his place in cyberspace should look.

He was in bed, reading, when there was a call from London. Cam listened, agreed to what was required of him, and then made a call to Valencia airport to book a seat on the first flight to Schipol where an onward ticket would be waiting for him.

He didn't need to pack. For years he had lived with a grip containing all he would need to survive wherever his masters sent him. Until the end of the year, that would continue. But once his present contract expired he would be a free agent. Whether it was too late for him to change from a nomad to a settler he couldn't tell, till he tried it.

Finally, he set his alarm clock to wake him in time to drive up the *autopista* to Valencia. Then he turned out the light and, with the ease of long habit, settled down to sleep.

*   *   *

When, checking her e-mail next morning, Liz read, 'Gotta go! Not sure when I'll be back. Will keep in touch if I can. *Adios*. Cam,' she should have felt relief that a threat to her peace of mind had been removed, if only temporarily.

What she actually felt was dejection.

The night before, on the Spanish teletext news that she read to improve her vocabulary, there had been an item about more than sixty journalists being killed in various trouble-spots during the year. It seemed a horrendously high casualty rate and she couldn't help thinking how dreadful it would be if, just when he was thinking about retiring, Cam's luck ran out.

A week went by with no word from him. By now she had carried out his instructions to do with his website and could do no more till she saw him again.

One glorious morning, when the weather was warmer than many summer days in England, as a change from walking through the vineyards she decided to explore one of the old mule tracks that led into the mountains. Now that mules had been replaced by rotavators, such tracks were used only by walkers and botanists.

She took an orange and some chocolate. After walking uphill for an hour, she ate them sitting on a rock with a panoramic view of the whole valley. It was on the way back that the accident happened. Looking at the view instead of the track, she trod on a wobbly piece of rock, lost her footing, and fell. If she hadn't flung out her arm in an instinctive effort to recover her balance, she would have escaped with bruises. But her outstretched hand took the brunt of the fall and the jarring impact was so agonising that she thought she might pass out.

For a moment she lay in a heap, convinced she had broken her arm and wondering how the hell she was going to get herself down the mountain. Then, knowing that she must, however difficult it might be, she struggled back to her feet. Fortunately it was not her elbow or her forearm that was damaged, only her rapidly swelling wrist.

By the time she got back to the village, the pain was becoming alarming. She had heard that the village had a *practicante*, a medical assistant who gave injections and changed dressings. But she didn't know where this person was to be found, and the building that housed the doctor's surgery was open only in the morning. She could ask at the *farmacia*, but she felt she needed a cup of tea and perhaps a slug of brandy before explaining the situation to the chemist in Spanish.

Then, as she turned the corner of her street, she was astonished to see Cam talking to the woman who lived opposite. For a moment she almost burst into tears of relief.

The woman spotted Liz first and, tapping his arm, pointed to her.

'You're back,' she said, forcing a smile as they met on her side of the street.

'Your neighbour has just been telling me that you went out several hours ago—' He noticed the hand she was holding against her chest. 'Liz…what's happened? What's wrong with your wrist?'

'I think I may have broken it. I was out walking and I fell. Would you mind explaining to the chemist? I don't know the words to—'

'The *farmacia* will be closed till four-thirty. The chemist won't be there until later. I'll run you over to Denia. If it's broken, it needs to be X-rayed and put in plaster. But first it needs a cold compress and a sling. Come to my place and I'll fix you up.'

'I don't want to be a nuisance…' she began.

'Don't be silly. Come on.' He put an arm round her waist as if he feared that without support she might collapse, and indeed she did feel rather wobbly. 'Tell me what happened.'

Liz explained. 'It was my own fault. I should have been looking where I was going.'

'Yes, one of the rules of mountain walking is ''look or walk, but don't try to do both'',' he agreed. 'But it's one that we've all forgotten one time or another. What you need is a cup of tea and a couple of painkillers.'

'When did you get back?' she asked.

'Less than an hour ago. Lucky I did. You couldn't drive with your left hand out of action.'

'There's a taxi service in Benimoro. I can get them to take me to Denia.'

'Certainly not. You need an interpreter with you. When people are hurt, or ill, they can't think straight.'

'I feel such a nuisance.'

'Well, don't. I have nothing else to do.'

By this time they had reached his front door. Still keeping his arm round her, he fished in his pocket for his key.

Half an hour later, they set out for the coastal town where there was a hospital. By this time Liz was feeling better, though still in considerable discomfort. A couple of paracetamol tablets had dulled the pain, and her forearm and hand were now in a triangular sling that Cam had produced from a well-stocked first aid box. Before fixing the sling he had applied a cold compress, inside a plastic bag, to her now grossly swollen wrist. She had been impressed by his efficiency. The village doctor could not have done more.

The drive to the hospital took about forty minutes, first by winding back roads and then by a section of the main road that followed the east coast of Spain all the way from the frontier with France to the naval base at Cartagena and beyond. Roughly parallel with it, the *autopista* offered a faster alternative, but was only practical for short journeys if the access points were convenient, which in this case they were not.

'From what I've heard, there can be very long delays in the accident and emergency department. I'm afraid you may have to hang about for ages,' said Liz, when they were nearly there.

'That's no problem. There's a paperback in the glove box if I need it.'

At the reception desk in the hospital's A&E department, it was Cam who explained in his fluent Spanish what had happened. Liz's details were noted and they were instructed to sit down and wait.

Almost immediately Cam was engaged in conversation by the woman on the other side of him. First she asked him about Liz's accident. Then she recounted, in detail, the circumstances that had brought her, and her injured daughter, to the hospital.

Listening to their conversation, but understanding only about a tenth of it, Liz was impressed by the way Cam responded to outpourings that could not really be of great interest to him. Perhaps, she thought, it was his ability to tune in to the wavelengths of many different kinds of people, from high-powered politicians to someone like the little woman next to him, whose work-worn hands and cheap clothes indicated that she had lacked most of life's privileges, that made him such a successful journalist.

From time to time someone in urgent need of attention arrived and was whisked through the door leading to the treatment rooms. Inevitably this slowed down the rate at which those in the waiting room were told to go through.

More than an hour passed before Liz was called. Cam rose to accompany her but was not allowed to enter the treatment section. There followed another long wait before her wrist was examined and she was told that her wedding ring, now very tight because of the swelling, would have to be cut off. Done with a special kind of clipper, this was not painful. Then her wrist was X-rayed.

Greatly to her relief, she was told that no bones were broken but the wrist was badly sprained and would need to be put in plaster. Again, she had to wait before her wrist was wrapped in gauze and plaster applied to the upper side only. At last, three hours after her arrival, she was free to return to the waiting room.

She found Cam chatting to a young man in a blue boilersuit who appeared to have nothing wrong with him so presumably had come with a workmate. As soon as he noticed Liz, Cam excused himself to his companion and joined her.

'It's not broken, only sprained,' she told him. 'They've told me to see my doctor, to have the plaster removed, in ten days. I'm terribly sorry you've had this long wait.'

'It hasn't seemed that long. The guy I've been chatting to is a telephone engineer. I picked up some interesting stuff from him. You must be starving. Before we go back, let's have a snack and some coffee...but not in the hospital's cafeteria where the queue for service is probably as long as it is here.'

He put his hand under the elbow of her right arm and, with his other hand, pushed the exit doors open for her.

It was when they were in a nearby *bar-restaurante*, drinking coffee and waiting for slices of tortilla to be heated in the microwave, that Cam noticed the absence of her wedding ring and concluded it had been cut off. But he didn't remark on it, guessing that it would have upset her to have the symbol of her marriage removed. He knew that some women never took their wedding rings off from a superstitious feeling that to do so was bad luck. Liz didn't seem that type but, often, people's natures were not all of a piece. He had come across sensible, down-to-earth personalities who, on closer acquaintance, had revealed all kinds of unexpected quirks.

While they were eating the tortilla, he said, 'What are you doing for Christmas, Liz?'

'I'm going to the UK to stay with my mother. Why do you ask?'

'I'm spending it with some friends at a *casa rural* about forty kilometres inland. Do you know about the *casas rurales*?'

'Only that the literal translation is country houses and that there's one in our village run by an English couple. But I haven't met them.'

'In the context of places to stay in the Spanish countryside, they vary from houses to rent to small, simple hotels. The one where my friends and I have booked rooms is run by a French couple whose cooking is excellent. There are only six bedrooms, four doubles and two singles. I thought, if you had nothing better to do, you might like to come with us.'

'It's kind of you to think of it. I wish I could accept. I'm not looking forward to returning to

English winter weather, or the hassle at Alicante airport.'

'Is your mother on her own?'

'No, my aunt shares the house with her since my parents separated. My father has moved to Florida with his American girlfriend.'

'My parents have split up too,' said Cam. 'They've both remarried people with grown-up children and grandchildren, so I don't feel it's necessary to play the dutiful son. Also I have my sisters to do the filial thing. Most years I've been abroad anyway. But if you are an only child, the ties are stronger.'

She said, 'Yes,' but made no other comment, and he had the intuitive feeling that it was her sense of duty rather than strong affection that was making her go back.

'Is it possible you'll have to cancel your plans and fly off somewhere this year?' she asked.

'Not this year. My contract has almost run out. I've made it clear I won't be available. You've booked your flight, I imagine? What day are you leaving?'

'I'm going for two weeks—December eighteenth to January first.'

'I'll run you to the airport.'

'I couldn't possibly put you to that trouble. You've done enough for me already. I'll go on the bus, or maybe that funny little train that runs between Denia and Alicante.'

'What time is your flight?'

'Not till early evening, so I have all day to get there.'

'I want to do some Christmas shopping in Alicante. Why don't we go down in the morning, browse in the two big department stores and have lunch at a restaurant I know? You won't get a memorable dinner on the plane, that's for sure.'

She gave him one of her doubtful looks. 'I didn't think men did Christmas shopping,' she said.

'Perhaps they don't if they have women to do it for them, but I haven't,' said Cam. 'Have you been to Alicante? Like Barcelona, it benefits from having a waterfront. Cities by the sea never seem as claustrophobic as inland cities.'

'I've never been into Alicante, only passed it on the motorway,' she told him.

'Then why not grab the chance to explore it, with me as your guide?' he said, smiling at her.

'All right...thank you...thank you very much.'

'Good, that's settled.'

That night, sitting beside the butane gas *estufa* that heated her sitting room when she did not want to light the logs inside the closed stove, Liz wished she was not committed to going to London for Christmas. She would much rather have joined Cam and his friends at the *casa rural*.

She wished she knew why he had suggested it. To be kind? It didn't seem likely he would go *that* far out of his way to befriend a new-comer to Spain, even one with whom he now had a professional involvement. He was paying her well for her services. Why would he feel the need to be friendly as well?

The longer she knew him, the more he was an enigma she could not fathom. Perhaps if she had not heard about his reputation, and had not seen for herself the kind of woman with whom he amused himself, she would have been able to judge him on the basis of his behaviour to-wards her. But the memory of him embracing Fiona by the bedroom window was hard to dis-miss.

Remembering the last time Duncan had made love to her, Liz looked down at the bare third finger on her left hand and sighed. Perhaps it would be possible to have the break in the ring mended, but she did not think she would do that. Already her marriage seemed as distant as her schooldays.

*　　*　　*

In the following week, Cam called at her house every day to see if she needed help with tasks that were hard or impossible with only one hand in use.

After a week, rather than going to the doctor, Liz decided to take off the plaster herself. It was a simple matter of cutting through the gauze bandaging on the underside of her wrist.

The next time Cam called and found her using both hands normally, he said, 'I've been meaning to talk to you about the inadvisability of wandering around in the mountains on your own. Earlier this year, an artist I know had an unpleasant experience while she was painting somewhere on Montgo, the mountain to the north of Jávea. Some guy appeared and started exposing himself. She's twenty years older than you are, but it scared her and she grabbed her equipment and made a dash for her car. I think she panicked unnecessarily. Flashers aren't usually a serious threat to women's safety. But, that said, they can be alarming. The other hazard of solitary hill-walking is running into a herd of cattle, including some *toros*.'

'Surely not the bulls used in bullfights?' Liz exclaimed in surprise. 'I thought they were bred in the south of Spain, not in these parts.'

'The most famous herds supplying bulls to the top-level fights are bred in the south,' he agreed. 'But all over Spain there are less important *corridas*, and many local *fiestas* have bull-running. Certain streets are closed off and the youths of the town show off in front of the girls. I've seen those beasts in the mountains.'

'Goodness…how scary. I had no idea they were wandering around loose up there. I'd rather meet a flasher than a bull any day,' Liz said, with feeling.

Cam laughed. 'The cattle aren't wandering around loose in the sense you mean. They graze as a group and sometimes there's a herdsman with them. Personally I wouldn't walk through the middle of a herd. The cows can be dangerous if they have young calves. But it's easy enough to skirt round them.'

'What if you were going up a track and they were on their way down?'

'Then the thing to do would be to get off the track till they'd passed. Probably the wisest thing, if you want to explore the mountains, is to join a walking group. There are plenty of them. If you had sprained your ankle instead of your wrist, getting back to base could have been a problem.'

That night Liz had a strange dream in which Deborah, her computer club friend, persuaded her to take the train from Alicante to Madrid to do some Christmas shopping. On arrival,

Deborah announced she had tickets for an important bull fight. Liz was reluctant to go. Although she knew that in Spain bull-fighting was regarded as an art form as well as a sport, she disliked the idea of animals being tormented for entertainment, even though the matadors also risked injury and death.

But Deborah overruled her objections and she found herself attending the fight at which the star turn was going to be a famous bullfighter called El Macho. When he appeared in the ring, he came straight to where Liz and Deborah were sitting. Looking up at Liz and speaking English, he said, 'You are the most beautiful woman here, *señorita*. If I bring you the bull's ears, will you reward me with a kiss?'

Before she could make up her mind what to answer, she woke up.

What disturbed her about the dream, and kept her awake for a long time, was that the matador had been Cam in a suit of lights.

The dream was still on her mind when, next day, she resumed her work in his garden. He had told her he was going to have lunch with a man who, during his professional life, had directed some fine documentaries and now, in retirement, lived somewhere inland from Gandia. Liz delayed her stint in the courtyard until she judged Cam had left the house.

To have dreamed about him troubled her. She did not want him invading her subconscious mind. Yet within a few minutes of thinking this, she found herself daydreaming about him: thinking how well a suit of lights would become him. As she knew from the pages of *Hola!*, the Spanish magazine which had inspired *Hello*, not all matadors were men of imposing stature, but even the short, stocky ones looked good in the traditional costume with its embroidered epaulettes, short jacket and tight-fitting britches.

Cam's broad shoulders and long legs needed no enhancement. They would set off the costume. In her mind's eye, she saw again him striding across the sand to the barricade in front of her seat, and the teasing glint in his eyes as he asked her to reward him with a kiss.

Stop it! she told herself angrily. Once before, a long time ago, her imagination had led her down dangerous paths into a world of misleading illusions. She was not going to let that happen a second time. For the rest of her life she would keep her feet firmly on the ground.

CHAPTER FOUR

Amar y saber, todo junto no puede ser

To love and to be wise are incompatible

ON THE day of her flight to England, they drove down the *autopista* to the provincial capital in Cam's new Mercedes. Previously he had rented cars, but now that he was going to be in Spain more often, he needed a car of his own.

Liz had never been a car-conscious person, but she had noticed Mercedes sports cars whenever they whipped past her because of their broad wheel-base and their look of being fast but safe.

'I like the sweeping curves of this road,' said Cam, as they headed south. 'There's a place on the shortcut from Valdecarrasca to the coast where you get a terrific view of the *autopista*, supported by tall columns, crossing a dry river valley. It's a masterpiece of engineering and artistry. In February, when the almond groves on either side of the backroad are in blossom, I must remember to photograph it for the website.'

106

'The almond blossom season is something I'm looking forward to,' said Liz. 'Spring in February is a concept that people who grow up in northern countries find it hard to get their mind round.'

'That reminds me, do you have a key-holder...someone in the village who could get into your house in your absence?'

'No, I don't. Should I?' she asked.

'It's a sensible precaution against unforeseen emergencies. The Drydens have a key to my house. If you like, I'll do the same for you. I don't suppose you have a spare key with you, but it wouldn't take long to get one cut in Alicante. One or both the department stores may have a key-cutting service.'

Sooner than Liz had expected, the city appeared on the skyline. Glancing at the speedometer, she realised that they had been travelling much faster than she had realised. The car's superior road-holding made it seem to be going more slowly than it was.

Although she had passed her test soon after her eighteenth birthday, and normally enjoyed being at the wheel, she would not have wanted to negotiate the streets of a busy city in a new and expensive vehicle. But Cam seemed unconcerned by Alicante's congested streets and one-way system. He drove along the waterfront, past the palm-lined pedestrian esplanade, before turning into the heart of the city where the pavements were crowded with fashionably dressed women and dapper men.

Living quietly in Valdecarrasca, Liz had forgotten what a city felt like. But in any case Alicante, under a cloudless blue sky with the sun shining, was very different from a typical December day in London. However, as far as the Spanish were concerned it was winter and many of the men were wearing smart overcoats and the women furs which here, it seemed, were still acceptable.

Cam parked the car in an underground parking lot belonging to El Corte Inglés, one of Spain's most famous department stores.

'I don't think they'd call it ''the English cut'' today,' he said dryly, as they entered the lift. 'A fashion journalist I know says the Germans have the edge for fine materials and tailoring. That's a very nice suit you're wearing—' with a downward glance at her classically simple fine wool jacket and skirt. 'Where was it made?'

'In Germany.' She would have travelled in something more casual but, because they were going to have lunch in the city, had decided to cut a dash. It was unlikely the suit would have many airings in future.

The last time Liz had gone shopping with a man had been with her father, an extravagant shopper who enjoyed chatting up pretty sales-girls. Duncan, indoctrinated by his mother, had regarded all shops as women's places. Uninterested in his appearance, he had even left it to Liz to pick out his suits.

She was curious to see what kind of shopper Cam was. Today he was wearing a long-sleeved light blue shirt and well-cut navy blue trousers with black socks and black calf loafers. On leaving the car, he had taken from the back seat a light-coloured sports coat. She knew by the way it fitted him that it had to be custom-made. No off-the-peg jacket would have fitted his shoulders and broad back so perfectly.

By lunch time they had toured the entire store and Liz had learnt a lot more about him. Unlike her father, he didn't flash numerous credit cards, nor did he ogle the female sales staff. It was they who looked appreciatively at him. Unlike her husband, he was obviously at ease in this environment, even on the fashion floors where he looked for gifts for the women he was spending Christmas with. He didn't ask Liz for advice, but picked out the presents himself, all of them things she would have been happy to receive.

At half past one, leaving their shopping to be picked up later, they strolled down to the esplanade she had glimpsed earlier. By now most of the benches were occupied by people chatting while others strolled back and forth. In a pavilion, a uniformed band played middlebrow music.

'Are you wilting? We should have had a coffee break,' said Cam. 'Our table is booked for two so there's time for a glass of wine in one of the pavement cafés, if we can find any free seats.'

'I'm not wilting. It's been great fun. What a beautiful pavement,' said Liz, indicating the tessellated marble surface they were walking on.

'Red, cream and black are the city's colours. This undulating design represents the waves of the sea,' he explained, looking towards the harbour.

He did not notice, as Liz did, a couple of expensively dressed women both looking him over and exchanging a glance that meant the Spanish equivalent of 'I wouldn't mind spending time with him!'

It was an unwelcome reminder that, although they might think her lucky to have such a personable man in tow, in fact he was only being neighbourly and she wasn't the type of woman he usually escorted.

'Quick...I've spotted some empty chairs.' He grabbed her arm to steer her to a nearby café where people were drinking *aperitivos*.

'Where does your mother live, Liz?' he asked, after a waiter had taken his order. When she told him, he said, 'Never been there.'

'You haven't missed much. It's the epitome of everything that's boring about the outer suburbs.'

'To a journalist, nowhere is boring. Suburbia is full of interesting stories and people.'

'Not in the street where my mother lives,' Liz said dryly. 'Respectability is the watchword.'

He gave her a penetrating look. 'But what about your mother's daughter, who broke out and went to Spain? I could get a story out of her, couldn't I?'

The waiter came back with two glasses of champagne and some little dishes of *tapas*.

'Couldn't I?' Cam persisted.

'I suppose an expert journalist can make a story out of almost anything. But even you would find it difficult. Coming to Spain isn't particularly adventurous. Thousands of people do it every year.'

'Yes, but most of the expats are retired. For someone of your age to come is a lot more enterprising.' He picked up his glass. 'I won't say Merry Christmas because it doesn't sound as if it will be merry for you. Let's drink to the New Year...and to our new directions.'

'To new directions,' she echoed.

As she drank some of the pale golden wine, it occurred to her that this was one of life's golden moments that she would remember when she was old.

The warm winter sunlight, the fronds of the palms stirred by a light breeze from the sea, the animated Spanish conversations going on around her, the personable man with whom she was sharing a table: all these combined to make a memory that would still be vivid half a century on, if she lived that long.

'Do you like *boquerónes*?' Cam asked, offering her a dish of pickled anchovies that, for easy eating, had been curled up and speared with toothpicks.

'Very much.' She took one. 'I like *albóndigas* too.' She looked at the small meatballs in a red sauce. 'Compared with Spanish nibbles, crisps and peanuts seem seriously boring.'

Presently, on the way to the restaurant, Cam produced from his pocket a rolled-up pale yellow tie. 'I'd better put this on. In the States, it's OK not to wear a necktie, as they call it, as long as you have a jacket. Here, except in the tourist resorts, they tend to be more formal.'

He threaded the tie under his shirt collar and tied it with the swift deft movements of long practice. Watching his lean brown fingers adjusting the knot, she felt a fluttering sensation that she recognised as excitement. She had read that champagne was an aphrodisiac, but surely one glass was not enough to kindle thoughts and feelings she would prefer to stay dormant? Closing her mind to them, she made herself pay attention to the shop windows they were passing.

Only a handful of people had arrived at the restaurant before them. While they were being shown to their table by the head waiter, they passed a table occupied by four Spanish businessmen of around Cam's age. Both the men seated on the outward-facing banquette gave Liz an interested glance that she felt was probably more attributable to her escort's charisma than to her own looks. Even off-screen, in a country where he wouldn't be widely recognised, Cam had the ineffable quality known as presence. When she was with him some of it rubbed off on her; waiters were more deferential, people who might have ignored her had she been alone looked at her with attention. It was a curious sensation to be caught in someone else's spotlight and she wasn't sure that she liked it.

By the time they had chosen their lunch and eaten their *montaditos*, the tempting morsels presented on little squares of toast, the restaurant was filling up with affluent Alicantinos. Seafood and savoury rice dishes were the mainstays of the menu here, and they both had a shrimp starter followed by *suquet de peix* which the head waiter translated as fisherman's pot.

'I hope you are going to let me share this,' said Liz, when Cam asked for the bill.

'Absolutely not,' he said firmly.

Seeing that it would be futile to argue, she said, 'Then at least let me contribute something towards the petrol and cost of the motorway.'

'I appreciate the offer...but no. I was going to come anyway. Your company has made it more enjoyable.'

It was said in a matter-of-fact tone, but she could not help feeling a glow of pleasure. 'It's been a wonderful meal. The whole day has been fun,' she said.

'Good. We must do it again.'

The rest of the afternoon passed as pleasantly as the morning. Soon it was time to drive to the airport on the southern outskirts of the city. There, in the car park, Liz transferred the presents bought for her mother and aunt to her suitcase and Cam wheeled it as far as the entrance of the departure section of the terminal.

There he set the case down and said, 'I'll say goodbye here. I may not be at home when you come back so I won't arrange to pick you up in case I can't make it.'

'You've been more than kind already. I'm very grateful. I hope you enjoy your stay at the *casa rural*. I *shall* wish you a Merry Christmas,' she said, smiling and offering her hand.

Cam took it, but then, to her surprise, he leaned forward and brushed a light kiss first on one cheek and then the other. 'Goodbye, Liz. Take care. See you soon.'

He released her hand and turned away, striding across the road where coaches, taxis and cars were allowed to put down and pick up their passengers to where he had left the Mercedes in the car park.

Liz watched him go in a daze of surprise and uncertainty. Kissing on meeting and parting was widely practised in Spain, and many of the expat community had adopted the habit and exchanged social kisses with each other at every opportunity, to an extent that she found rather absurd. But she had not expected Cam to kiss her goodbye and, if she had, would not have expected the commonplace gesture to give her such a buzz.

Her parents had not been demonstrative with each other. She had never seen them embrace.

Nor had Duncan and his family been given to affectionate gestures. As far back as she could remember, Liz had wanted to hug and be hugged but had adapted herself to the ways of the people closest to her. That was one of the reasons why not having a baby had been such a disappointment. With a child she could have acted on her impulses. Babies and toddlers enjoyed being cuddled and kissed.

Inside the terminal, she joined the long line of passengers waiting to check in for her flight. It was forty minutes before she reached the desk, was given her boarding card and could take the escalator to the departure lounge level where there was also a cafeteria and a shop selling papers and paperbacks. Liz had a look at the books but did not buy one as she meant to spend the flight planning the site she would need as a website designer. It would be separate from the site that showcased her skills as a crafts designer.

Having coffee in the café reminded her of the previous occasions when she had flown back to England from this airport. The first three times had been after holidays with her in-laws at the villas they had rented in Denia, Moraira and Altea. The last time had been after she had flown down to sign the papers that made her the owner of Beatrice Maybury's house.

At the outset, she would have preferred to go further afield, to the Greek islands or to Italy. But Duncan, who had been careful with money, had seen staying with his parents as a useful saving. It had never crossed her mind that she might one day live here. Or that a few years hence another man's kiss on her cheek would make her heart beat as fast as when, in her early teens, she had said shy hellos to the son of the new people next door when he and she happened to be in their parents' back gardens at the same time.

Presently, sitting in the departure lounge— perhaps the only person there who was looking forward to the return flight more than to the outward flight—Liz thought about Cam's toast to 'new directions'.

The year that would soon be ending had been a momentous one for her. Would next year be even more life-changing?

Her mother, Mrs Bailey, and her aunt, Mrs Chapman, were both television addicts. The small set in the kitchen was switched on before breakfast and, except when they were out shopping, the big new set in the lounge remained on till they went to bed. They planned their day's viewing as carefully as people preparing for an expedition. When there was a gap between their many favourite programmes, they filled it with a video of a programme that had conflicted with something they liked even better.

Television had taken over their lives, Liz realised. She had no quarrel with that, if it kept them happy. But it drove her mad. There were times when she had to escape by going for a walk even though the weather was terrible.

She was herself an addict of another kind, she discovered, during the first week with them. Without e-mail and the Web, her life had lost an important dimension. After seven days without a 'fix', she was driven to buying herself a laptop.

She justified this expensive outlay by telling herself that it was unprofessional to depend on her desktop computer. She needed to have a backup machine. But she knew that the real reason was that, if Cam e-mailed her while she was out of Spain, she wanted to be able to pick up his message and perhaps reply. That she could have accessed her mailbox from a cyber café was something she chose to ignore.

'Is it OK if I plug my computer into the telephone jack?' she asked her mother, after unwrapping the laptop in her bedroom. 'You aren't expecting any important calls in the next half-hour, are you?'

'The only person who rings me is you,' said Mrs Bailey. 'I don't know what the world's coming to. People are lucky to see their children once a year these days. Families used to be close.'

Liz was tempted to say, But now that I am here you don't want to talk to me. You're more interested in your favourite presenters' lives than in mine. But she knew that, even though it was true, to say so would hurt her mother's feelings. Instead, she said, 'It's nice that you and Auntie Sue are still bosom buddies. Not all sisters get on as well as you two.'

'We have to, don't we? If we relied on our children where would we be? You've gone off to Spain, and Sue's two hardly ever visit her.'

Between them, Liz's cousins had five children. 'You haven't room to put them up and they can't afford to stay at a hotel. Why not go and visit them...or come and stay with me?' she suggested.

'You know I'm not keen on flying.' Mrs Bailey caught sight of the clock. 'Oh...it's almost time for Oprah.' Her expression brightened. Of all her television idols, the American chat show hostess topped the list. 'Sue, hurry up, dear. Oprah's starting,' she called from the doorway.

*   *   *

Liz's homeward flight was delayed by two hours, but she didn't mind. She liked airports. It was drizzling when the plane took off from Gatwick, but the sun was shining at Alicante. She took a taxi to the coach station in the city and, after half an hour's wait, climbed on a bus that would drop her off at a town not far from Valdecarrasca. There she could call another taxi to take her the last ten kilometres.

She enjoyed the bus journey with its views of the mountains through the offside windows and nearside glimpses of the blue Mediterranean and the coastal towns.

'The topless towers of Benidorm,' Cam had said sardonically, as they drove past the high-rise blocks of the famous resort a fortnight earlier.

She had known it was a literary reference and in England had looked it up and found it was part of a poem about Helen of Troy.

Was this the face that launch'd a thousand ships,
And burnt the topless towers of Ilium?
Sweet Helen, make me immortal with a kiss!

Reading it, she had wondered if Cam would ever meet a woman who would have the effect on him that Helen, wife of a king, had had on the prince who abducted her. Was Cam capable of that kind of overwhelming passion?

She could not help being disappointed at receiving no e-mails from him during her absence. Now he was probably away, as he had said he might be. But even if he was not there, she looked forward to seeing the garden after a fortnight's absence. Her trip had proved one thing: the village was 'home'. Any lingering doubts about the wisdom of her decision to uproot herself had evaporated.

There was only one letter in the metal box attached to the wall beside Liz's front door. The envelope had no stamp. An unfamiliar hand had written 'Mrs Harris' and, in the bottom right-hand corner of the expensive envelope, 'By hand'.

Liz stuck it in the pocket of her jacket to be looked at after she had unlocked the front door and lifted her book-heavy suitcase over the threshold. When she and her luggage were inside, her first task was to open the curtains and let in some light. It was only then that she noticed a small parcel on the table that had not been there when she left home. For a moment or two she was baffled by how it could have got there. Then she remembered the spare key she had had cut in Alicante and given to Cam.

Wrapped in plain brown paper fastened with transparent sticky tape, the parcel was roughly the size of a 500 *gramos* box of *margarina*, but considerably heavier. Inside the outer wrapping were several layers of tissue that, unfolded, revealed an object that Liz had often admired when she saw it on the front doors of the more opulent Spanish town-houses.

Formed in the shape of a woman's hand emerging from a lace cuff, the brass door-knocker was clearly an antique, not one of the cheap reproductions she had sometimes seen for sale at junk markets. Probably this one had come from an old house that had been demolished. Cam could not have given her anything that would have delighted her more.

Taped to the back of the knocker was a card on which he had written—

Hope you like this. If so I'll fix it for you when I get back on Jan 4th. Happy New Year. Cam.

The news that in three days' time La Higuera would have its blinds up made her feel even more cheerful.

Valdecarrasca had two small general stores of the type that, in England, when she was a child, had been known as 'corner shops'. Like that of their now largely vanished counterparts in the UK, the village shopkeeper's livelihood was under threat from the supermarkets. But for the time being they were surviving and Liz made a point of using them.

It was not until after she had been to the shop run by Maria, a forty-something mother of several children, that Liz remembered the letter she had put in her pocket. She fished it out and slit the envelope. The letter inside was typewritten but topped and tailed in the same elegant hand that had addressed the envelope.

Dear Liz (if I may?)
Cam has told us how well you are looking after his garden. I am also an enthusiastic gardener. We are having a party for friends on January 4th and should be delighted if you can join us? Buffet supper. Smart casual. 8 p.m. If you can't make it, please ring me.
Hoping you will be free, Leonora Dryden.

The following morning, Liz put a note accepting the invitation in Mrs Dryden's letter box. For the rest of the day, at odd moments, she wondered what she should wear.

It was Deborah, her friend at the computer club, who told her about the nearly-new shop in

Denia where the wealthy expats who lived in the urbs on the coast disposed of their cast-offs.

Liz had first heard someone say 'urb' while staying with her parents-in-law. It was short, she discovered, for *urbanización*, the Spanish word for the clusters of villas that had sprung up like colonies of mushrooms wherever the land near the sea could be built on and now were spreading relentlessly inland.

'Why don't we go together?' Deb suggested. 'After we've shopped, we can lunch. There's no point in taking two cars. There must be somewhere on the main coast road where you can leave yours for a few hours while we drive the rest of the way in mine.'

The outing was a success. They both emerged from the nearly-new shop with bulging recycled carrier bags. As they finished lunch at a restaurant close to the sea's edge, Deborah said, 'Let's not go back the way we came. Let's go by the mountain road. You haven't been over Montgo yet, have you? There's a lovely view from the flat bit on top of the seaward end.'

The mountain called Montgo, its skirts now dotted with villas, was a major landmark along this stretch of the coast. Liz had assumed the only way round it was on the inland side. She had not known there was a winding road over the mountain connecting the town of Denia with the neighbouring small port of Jávea. She wondered if Cam knew about it and supposed he must. Uneasily aware that thoughts of him kept popping into her head with increasing frequency, she was also conscious that the uncharacteristically dropdead dress she had just bought had been chosen to stop him in his tracks rather than to cut a dash with the Drydens or their other guests.

'I wonder if you'll meet anyone interesting at this party you're going to?' said Deborah, as she drove round the tight hairpin bends ascending the mountain. 'If there are any eligible singles in this area, I never meet them.'

'Do you want another man in your life?' Liz asked.

'I certainly don't want a dud like the last one I had, but I'm over that fiasco now and, yes, I'd like to try again. Chance would be a fine thing,' Deborah added dryly.

At the top of the mountain road, but still well below the actual summit, a byroad led to the lighthouse at the seaward end of the massive promontory. There Deborah parked the car and they got out and strolled about.

'I guess it's different for you,' said Deborah. 'If someone has been happily married and then lost their partner through an accident, as you did, it must take longer to recover than from a marriage like mine that started going downhill almost from the end of the honeymoon.'

Liz liked Deborah and valued their friendship. But she didn't really want to get into in-depth discussions about their personal lives. 'Maybe a slow decline is more painful than a sudden ending,' she said. 'I can't say that living alone for the rest of my life bothers me. I'd rather be single than married to the wrong person.'

'I'm not going to argue with that!' Deborah said emphatically. 'But hopefully I'm wiser as well as older. Next time I won't lose my head as well as my heart.'

Later, when Deborah had dropped her off near her own car, and she was driving back to Valdecarrasca, Liz thought how easy it was, on the basis of insufficient evidence, to make false assumptions about people. She had probably done it herself. Maybe one day she would correct Deborah's assumption about her. Or maybe not. Usually it was better to let sleeping dogs lie.

On the afternoon of the party, she gave herself a top-to-toe beauty treatment starting with a luxuriously long bath and finishing with a pedicure and manicure.

From time to time she looked out of her kitchen window to see if the *persianas* at La

Higuera were up. At sunset they were still down. Perhaps Cam's return had been postponed for some reason.

Normally she picked up e-mails every two hours. At six o'clock the Inbox was empty. At seven, half an hour before starting to dress, she logged on and checked again. Nothing. Why should he let her know he wasn't coming? she asked herself. They were neighbours and business associates, not close friends. But she couldn't help feeling miffed that he hadn't made any contact since kissing her goodbye at the airport almost three weeks ago.

Before taking the new-to-her dress out of the wardrobe, she put on a new bra and briefs and a pair of sheer black tights. Then she spent twenty minutes putting on a party face and adding sheen to her newly washed hair with a tiny amount of wax spread on her palms.

Tonight was only the second time she had tried on the dress since Deborah's comment, 'That looks stunning on you,' had convinced her she had to buy it. Even second-hand, it hadn't been cheap. But, according to the shop's owner, the name on the satin label was that of a top German designer famous for mannishly tailored day clothes and glamorously feminine evening wear.

Carefully, Liz opened the zipper, and gathering the delicate folds of the exquisite fabric dropped them carefully over her head and helped them to slide down her body, the silk lining cool on her bare flesh.

When she looked at her reflection in the long mirror that was one of her additions to the house, she knew that tonight she was going to do something she had never done before. She was going to make an entrance.

The church clock was striking eight for the second time when she locked her front door and, with her red shawl protecting her upper body from the after-dark fall in temperature, walked to the Drydens' house, the sound of her heels echoing in the empty streets.

At that moment Cam's Mercedes was alongside the toll-booth at the *autopista* outlet nearest to Valdecarrasca. It had been a long day. Tired, and with things on his mind, he was not really in the mood for Leonora's chatfest. But he knew she had invited Liz and, as he was the only person she would know, he felt an obligation to show up. The Drydens' parties could be a bit of an ordeal for anyone who was shy or reserved and Leonora would be too busy hostessing to keep a close eye on the newest addition to what, by expat social standards, was a fairly glittering circle.

By the time he closed his garage door it was nearly eight-thirty and he needed a shower and shave. But he was used to quick changes.

The clock was starting to strike nine when he left the house. In Spain, many foreigners arrived late in the belief that it was the custom here. Normally punctual himself, when he gave a party he expected people to show up at or close to the time he had decreed.

Knowing that the door would be open, he chose not to ring the bell that would require someone to break off their conversation to admit him. Letting himself in, he unwound his cashmere scarf and tossed it onto a dark oak hall chest. Then he climbed the stairs to the first-floor living room that had even better views of the valley than his own upper rooms.

About thirty people were drinking and chatting, but the space was large and lofty enough to prevent the noise level from becoming annoying. He took a sweeping look round, recognising most of the faces but not all. He didn't know the man who was chatting up a woman with beautiful legs and a silky fall of hair that half hid her profile.

Then she turned slightly towards where Cam was standing, at the same time lifting her hand to tuck the hair behind her ear. As she made that quintessentially feminine gesture, he experienced two reactions. First he recognised her. Then he remembered the feel of her cheek under his lips and felt a surging desire to kiss her again, on the mouth.

Liz was listening to the man called Tony who was her hostess's house guest when, suddenly, she had the feeling that someone was staring at her.

'Let me get you another drink,' said Tony, taking her glass. 'I'll be right back.'

She thought it was actually he who wanted a refill. His departure left her free to glance round the room. She found that someone *was* staring. It was Cam, standing by the double doors, fixing her with such a strange intense look that, for the first time that evening since she had put on the dress, she felt her confidence falter and was shaken by nervousness.

He came towards her, not smiling but extending his hand. When she gave him hers, he turned it and kissed it. Straightening, he said, 'You look beautiful.'

'Thank you.' Her self-possession returned. 'I'm glad you got back in time for the party.'

'Who is the guy with the moustache?'

'He's staying with Mr and Mrs Dryden. He's a professor of linguistics.'

'Interesting?'

'Extremely. How was your trip?'

'The weather was vile…snow turning to slush. How was yours?' he asked.

'I was pleased to get back. You must be longing for a drink. Don't let me stop you heading for the bar.'

'Is that a diplomatic way of telling me I've arrived in the middle of a promising tête-à-tête that you'd rather was not interrupted?'

'Not at all. I think you'd have more in common with Tony than I do. Language is your stock in trade. I'm better with visuals than words. Here he comes now. I'll introduce you.'

Soon after the two men started chatting, Leonora joined them. 'Delighted you made it, Cam.' She gave him a glass of red wine and offered a dish of smoked salmon and caviare *montaditos* to all three of them. 'I hope you don't mind if I whisk Tony away. There's someone I specially want him to meet.'

'Leonora has the most efficient antennae of any hostess I've met,' said Cam, as she led the other man away. 'I'm sure she knew that, after a trying day, I would rather talk to my ravishing neighbour than to the most brilliant professor in the whole of the US.'

'You promised not to flirt with me,' Liz reminded him.

'I promised to wait for a signal. You can't wear a dress like that and not expect to receive compliments. You should emerge from your chrysalis and shake out your wings more often. Why hide those legs inside trousers?' He stepped back the better to admire them.

'How many drinks did you have on the plane?' she asked.

'None. I never drink on flights if I have to drive when I land. This is my first alcohol today.'

She remembered that, in Alicante, he had had champagne before lunch but not much wine with their meal, and he had not been driving back until several hours later.

'I wonder what time we're eating?' he said. 'I skipped the inflight meal and my stomach is starting to growl.'

'I think supper proper starts at nine-thirty, but there are masses of nibbles. Wait here. I'll fetch a selection.'

But when she attempted to leave him, he caught her hand and made her stay. 'I can wait another fifteen minutes.'

'Oh…I've forgotten to thank you for the door-knocker,' Liz exclaimed. 'It was such a lovely surprise…my best Christmas present.'

Cam was still holding her hand. 'Then how about showing your pleasure in the traditional way?' He leaned towards her, offering a closely shaven cheek.

She didn't want to but, without seeming ungracious, she had no choice but to comply with the suggestion. As she pursed her lips, intending the kiss to be very brief and light, he turned his head and it was their mouths that made contact.

Angry that he had trapped her into a public gesture that must, if anyone noticed it, give a misleading impression that they were on much closer terms than was actually the case, Liz jerked back and gave him a glare.

'That wasn't fair,' she muttered crossly.

Yet, even as she reproached him, all her senses were tingling and sparking in the same way that a hand that had gone to sleep started coming back to life when its blood supply was restored. Feelings almost forgotten, because it was so many years since they had been experienced, revived with disturbing force.

Almost twenty years on, she relived the misleading rapture of her first kiss and all the passionate, only dimly understood longings it had aroused in her.

'Life isn't fair,' said Cam, her hand still imprisoned in his.

'Ladies and gentlemen, supper is served.' The ringing voice of their host broke the tension between them.

Moments later, a voice said, 'Cam, darling...long time no see,' and a woman in a purple top and dangling amethyst earrings began an animated monologue about the dramas in her life that allowed Liz to extricate her hand and remove herself from his orbit.

By the time supper was over, she had decided that the only way to deal with him was to stay resolutely unfazed. He was only trying it on. He wouldn't force himself on her. Not if he wanted to keep her as his garden-minder and website designer.

She must cultivate a light-hearted, 'down boy' manner, treating him like an over-exuberant dog. There was, she thought acidly, no shortage of accommodating bitches to waggle their tails invitingly at him. The woman he was talking to now was fifty if she was a day, but it was plain from the other side of the room that she would be more than willing to have an enjoyable fling with him.

Liz and another guest were in their hostess's bedroom, touching up their lipstick, when Mrs Dryden joined them. With her slim athletic figure and thick blonde hair, seen from behind she could pass for a much younger woman than she was. But her wrinkles, her neck and her liver-spotted hands indicated that she was in her late sixties or possibly older. Clearly colouring her hair was the only artifice she was prepared to use to keep age at bay.

She was simply dressed in a black satin shirt and black trousers with grosgrain ribbon down the side seams.

After chatting for a few minutes, she said, 'Liz, I have a gardening magazine I think would interest you. Come to my den and I'll find it for you.'

Her den was divided into three areas. On a large table stood a sewing machine. In another corner stood an easel with the charcoal outline for a portrait on canvas on it. There was also a writing desk and, nearby, a comfortable sofa backed by shelves for books and magazine boxes.

'Perhaps you already subscribe to *Gardens Illustrated*?' she said, closing the door behind them.

'No, I don't.'

'If you like it, I can lend you all my back numbers. But I thought the issue dealing with courtyards might give you ideas for Cam's and your own. Do sit down while I look for it.'

'Obviously you don't have a problem filling your time here, Mrs Dryden.'

'Do call me Leonora. No, certainly not. My problem is the reverse…finding time for all my pursuits. Ah, here it is.' She handed Liz a glossy magazine. 'What a gorgeous dress you're wearing. Cam mentioned that you have connections with a women's magazine. Were you the fashion editor?'

Liz laughed and shook her head. After explaining what she had done, she said, 'Actually I found this dress in a second hand shop in Denia. When it was new it would have been too expensive for me. I can't understand its original owner not keeping it. I shall wear it for ever.'

'Alas, there will come a time when you won't be able to,' said Mrs Dryden. 'There comes a point when arms are better covered up. But it will be at least twenty years before you reach that stage. I often sigh over clothes that I could have worn at your age but can't any more. Still, I have kept my waist, which is something to be thankful for. Have you ever been painted?'

'Not since primary school when we all did drawings of each other,' said Liz.

'I should like to paint you in that dress. Could you spare the time? It would take several hours but we could split them into forty-minute sessions. I find that's about my limit for intense concentration.'

'I'd be happy to pose,' said Liz.

'Good: I'll call you next week and we'll look at our diaries. Now, I think we'd better rejoin the others. Leave the magazine under your shawl on my bed.'

When they returned to her sitting room, she introduced Liz to some people she hadn't yet met, their chief interest in life being Spanish wild flowers, particularly the native plants.

Several times, while she was with them, she noticed Cam moving about the room, doing his guestly duty of mixing. His popularity was obvious, not only with women but also, a little surprisingly, with the men present. But the fact that he was a womaniser didn't necessarily make him a poacher of other men's women, she thought. Anyway it was unlikely he would pursue women past the first flush when voluptuous beauties like Fiona were available to him.

Being an early riser and unaccustomed to late nights, by half past eleven she was beginning to wilt. But as no one else seemed ready to leave, she waited until an elderly couple departed before seizing the opportunity of the Drydens' being together to thank them for having her and say goodnight.

'Allow me to walk you home,' said Tony, appearing beside them as they were shaking hands.

Had Leonora signalled to him? Liz wondered. She said, 'Thank you, but it isn't necessary. I don't mind walking through the village at night. There are no muggers here.'

'I will see Liz to her door,' said Cam, from behind her. *'Con permiso,'* he added, with a glinting glance that challenged her to refuse permission.

CHAPTER FIVE

Galan atrevido, de las damas preferido

A bold lover is a favourite with women

'GOOD party, didn't you think?' he said, as they left the house.

'Very good. A lovely house. Great food. Lots of interesting people. But I don't know what they will make of my little cottage when I ask them back.'

'They'll like it. Money and status symbols mean nothing to the Drydens. What they value are brains and initiative...and good manners,' he added. 'I'm sure you will write to Leonora tomorrow, but guests who don't are not invited again. She's a stickler for the old-fashioned courtesies.'

'I do know how to behave in polite society,' said Liz, rather miffed by the possibility that his comment had been a hint in case she did not. 'When you have time to look through your snail mail, you'll find a note I wrote to thank you for your Christmas present.' He would also find the

139

book she had bought for herself but decided to give to him.

'Are you still cross with me?' he asked.

'Not in the least. Why should I be?'

'Because I kissed you in public. It was only a peck...not enough to start any gossip.'

'Gossip doesn't need a solid foundation. It can start from nothing,' she retorted. 'But I should think my reputation is a good deal more robust than yours.'

'I agree with you,' he said carelessly. 'But gossip always exaggerates. I'm not as black as I'm painted. You have nothing to fear from me.'

'I didn't think I had.'

By the light of a street lamp, she saw the lines down his cheeks deepen, betraying amusement. 'You have a short memory, Liz. But I'm glad you've revised the opinion you held the first time we lunched. How about lunch tomorrow? I have another proposal I'd like to discuss with you.'

'It's my turn to stand you a lunch.'

'All right. We'll do it your way. What time do you want me to be ready?'

'Half past twelve, if that suits you. The restaurant is about half an hour's drive from here.'

By now they had reached her house. Liz had already taken her key from her evening bag. When Cam held out his palm, she put the key

on it and watched him unlock the door. Would
he try to kiss her goodnight? she wondered.
Would she let him? Or would she resist?

She did not find out because he did not attempt it.

'*Buenas noches…hasta mañana.*'

When he spoke Spanish, even commonplace
remarks like 'goodnight' and 'until tomorrow'
sounded oddly caressing.

'*Buenas noches.*' She watched him turn and
walk back the way they had come, his tall figure
casting a long shadow ahead of him.

After the warmth of the Drydens' sitting
room, her house felt like a dungeon. She hurried
upstairs to the bathroom where a hot towel rail
and an electric radiator, which she always
switched on at sundown, provided a comfortable
level of warmth. Her bedroom did not have a
heater, but the bed itself would be cosy because
she had put the electric blanket on before she
went out.

Before she took off her dress, she looked at
herself in the mirror behind the handbasin. 'You
look beautiful,' Cam had said. No other man
had ever said that to her. She had received lesser
compliments, but never that ultimate accolade,
and said in a tone that sounded as if he meant
it.

*   *   *

In the morning, Liz regretted agreeing to lunch with Cam. She shouldn't have drunk so much wine. It had clouded her judgment, she told herself severely.

After hand writing a thank-you letter to Leonora Dryden, she typed and printed her weekly letter to her mother.

Describing the party, she wrote, 'One of the guests was a television reporter, Cameron Fielding.' She had not told her mother he lived in the village or that she looked after his garden.

Later she put the first letter in the Drydens' box and posted the second in the yellow box attached to a wall in the main square.

Cam was already in the street outside his house when she arrived in her car. He was chatting to one of his neighbours, a small woman dressed in black, a convention still observed by many of the older ladies. This one had bandy legs, usually a sign that their owner had been born in the Thirties when Spain's civil war had made worse the poverty endured by most of the population in the first half of the last century.

As she slowed down, Liz saw that Cam was listening with the same close attention he had given to the well-heeled guests at the party. Clearly, like his hosts, he did not rate people according to their social status but by a yardstick of his own. There were some things about him that she liked very much, Liz thought, as she stopped the car a few yards short of them.

Perhaps the old lady was deaf and had not heard the car pull up. She had been in full spate for several more minutes and might have gone on indefinitely when he said something that made her pause and turn round. From their gestures, Liz gathered that the old lady was apologising for delaying him, and he was assuring her no apology was necessary.

'I wish my Spanish was good enough to talk to people the way you do,' she said, when he climbed in beside her.

'It will be. Give yourself time. Señora Mora was telling me about her brother who, when times were bad here, emigrated to Argentina and did well for himself.'

That he knew the Spanish woman's name and didn't refer to her as 'that old dear' sent him up another notch in her estimation.

When they were clear of the village, she said, 'Tell me about your new project.'

'If you don't mind I'd rather wait till we get to where we're going.'

'I hope it lives up to my friend's recommendation. I haven't been there before.'

'If we don't like it, we can always push on.' His tone was relaxed.

Half an hour later, they were the only patrons at a small country restaurant. This establishment was far more rustic than the one where he had taken Liz. Here, in the middle of nowhere, the place was run by a middle-aged woman and her mother. Inside the building were several long trestle tables, outside four metal tables. As it was a lovely day they chose to sit outside.

Cam filled their glasses from a jug of red *vino de mesa* they had seen filled from a cask inside the restaurant. 'It'll take them a while to cook our *paella* so I'll do my presentation now, shall I?'

'I wish you would. I'm seething with curiosity.'

'Have a swig of wine before I start. This could come as a slight shock.' He drank from his own glass. 'Mmm...this is good. I wonder where it comes from?'

'What could come as a shock?' Liz demanded impatiently.

'I think we should get married,' he told her calmly. 'When, last night, I called it a proposal, that's exactly what I meant. You and I have a lot to offer each other.

'Before you tell me I'm mad, let me explain my view of marriage,' he went on. 'I've seen a lot of marriages go wrong, including my parents', and a few that have been successful. The successful ones all seem to have a common denominator. They are basically intimate friendships between people prepared to make trade-offs. In marriages that last, both partners will give up something they want if it will benefit their partner. But it has to work both ways. It's no use one person making all the sacrifices.'

By now Liz was recovering from her initial stupefaction.

'I'm sure all that's true,' she said, 'but I can't relate it to us. We hardly know each other. We come from completely different backgrounds. We have different temperaments. We—'

He cut her short. 'Let's take those first three items and deal with the others later. You feel we hardly know each other. What does a woman need to know about a man before she marries him? Take five minutes to think about it and then tell me your conclusions.'

Wine glass in hand, he rose from his chair and strolled across the rough turf to where the land fell away so that from where she was sitting Liz could only see the distant sea with the Peñon de Ifach rising out of it.

Marriage, she thought, still dazed. Marriage. Why should he offer me, of all people, the thing that he has never offered to any of those other women?

Or maybe he has, and the one he wanted refused him. Could that be the reason he has played the field so intensively? Because someone has broken his heart?

She looked at his long straight back, the taut backside and the set of his head on his neck. Physically, everything about him was attractive. But what was he like inside?

Presently Cam came back. 'Have you worked it out?'

She nodded. 'I think so. She needs to know that he's kind, that he has a sense of humour, and that he won't bore her.' There was a fourth essential—that he was a considerate lover—but it wasn't something she could discuss with him.

'And how do I rate?'

'You rate well...as far as I can tell. But I think it takes time to be sure...more time than we've known each other.'

The younger of the two women came out with a basket of bread, a bowl of olives and a dish of mussels, their black shells piped with what looked like fine squiggles of icing sugar but what turned out to be a corraline trail left on them by some other sea creature.

'Do you like mussels?' Cam asked. They had not been offered a choice of starters, only the option to have lamb chops or paella for their main course.

'I don't know. I've never tried them before. They're a beautiful colour.' Before she ate, she added, 'This is all pretty basic compared with the restaurants you took me to. But my friend said it was a glimpse of the way Spain used to be, before it was colonised by northerners. But of course you were here as a schoolboy so you know what it was like then.'

He said, 'But now I am a man who has missed a lot of the best things life has to offer, and who wants to make up for lost time. Liz, I don't want to seem intrusive, but were you and your husband childless by choice or chance?'

'Certainly not by choice. We both wanted children, but it wasn't possible. Duncan had had orchitis in his teens. His family doctor didn't warn him that, occasionally, it leaves men infertile.' Though she had always suspected that Duncan's possessive mother had known it was a possibility. 'Not that it would have made any difference if we had known. I loved him. I would have married him regardless.'

'"Love is not love which alters when it alteration finds...O, no! it is an ever-fixed mark",' Cam quoted.

For a moment she was tempted to confide in him. Instead she said, 'There's no guarantee that I can have children now. I passed all the tests at the time, but it was a long time ago and the chances don't get better as women get older.'

'You're not that old,' he said, smiling. 'Lots of women don't start their families until forty is on the horizon. The pattern of life has changed since our parents' time. I know a number of couples who've decided not to have children. They feel procreation should be an option, not a convention. I agree with that point of view. But, for myself, I'd like to have a crack at parenthood.'

'Is that your main reason for deciding to marry?'

'Certainly not. If I arranged my reasons in order, it would be well down the list.'

'What would come first?'

He drank some wine before he answered. 'Two things: companionship and sex. Someone to share my thoughts and my bed.'

'Rumour says there's never been any shortage of bed partners.'

'Rumour tends to exaggerate. I'm not denying that my past has not been monastic, but that doesn't mean I'm incapable of fidelity in a permanent relationship.'

'Don't you think you might get bored in a permanent relationship?'

'No, I don't. I'm not bored by my favourite books, my favourite music, my favourite paintings. While I hope to go on making new friends for the rest of my life, I don't expect to lose interest in my first close friends.' He paused. 'To be blunt about it, freewheeling girls like Fiona were a pleasant expedient while I was footloose, with a good chance of being blown to bits. You may think that reprehensible, but making love is a fundamental human need. You married young. If you hadn't, are you sure you wouldn't have had some pleasant but temporary relationships while you waited for a permanent partner to show up?'

'I expect I might have,' she agreed. 'Though I can't imagine ever going to bed with anyone unless I had *some* feelings for them...unless I had hopes that it would last. But, I suppose, if you're in a job that involves serious risks you probably look at it differently...the way people do in wartime. Live for today in case there is no tomorrow.'

'Well, as you know better than most, tomorrow is never a sure thing for anyone. But I'm certain that your husband, if he could have foreseen the premature ending of his life, would not have wanted you to spend the rest of yours in mourning for him.' Cam said quietly. 'Romantic love isn't the only basis for a successful marriage, you know. In a lot of cultures it starts as a practical arrangement and affection grows on the way along.'

'But not in our culture.'

'Our culture is in the melting pot. Who can say where it's heading? I think we are all on the threshold of enormous, exciting changes. I also think you and I would enjoy them more if we faced them together.'

At this point the restaurant's owner came out to collect their plates and the dish of empty shells and squeezed halves of lemon.

'*Bien?*' she enquired.

'*Muy bien, señora.*' Cam chatted to her as easily as if the conversation she had interrupted had been of no special consequence.

Did he take it for granted that she would accept his proposal? Liz wondered. But really why should he not? He had a great deal to offer. There must be any number of women who, given the chance, would jump at becoming Mrs Cameron Fielding, wife of a well-known man who was also exceptionally attractive. He was everything most women dreamed of, except that he didn't believe in love and perhaps was incapable of feeling it.

'Have you never been in love?' she asked, when they were alone again.

'Yes…in my youth…of course,' he said, looking amused. 'Between seventeen and twenty-three I fell in love several times, but fortunately the girls didn't feel the same way or their parents intervened.'

'Fortunately?'

He shrugged. 'I didn't see it as fortunate at the time, but I do now. Generally speaking people in their teens and early twenties are far too immature to embark on a serious relationship. They need to find out who they are before they can tell who will suit them for the rest of their lives. You may have known who you were when you got married, but most people don't till much later.'

'I'm not sure I know who I am even now,' she said, in a wry tone. 'Life seems to happen to me. I don't feel I'm in control.'

'You made the decision to come here, to make a fresh start.'

'It was more of an impulse than a considered decision...something that happened by chance rather than by design. I didn't decide in advance that I wanted to live abroad.'

'Well, now there is a decision to make and I think we should fix a time limit. I'll give you until the mimosa in my garden comes out. What could be more romantic?' he said, with a teasing smile.

'When does that happen?' She had heard there were seven varieties of mimosa growing in Spain, some flowering earlier than others.

'Depends...usually in March, but sometimes earlier if the winter has been particularly mild. Meantime we can spend a lot of time together and do an in-depth check for incompatibilities.'

'I can spot one big one already. You take the idea of marriage a lot less seriously than I do,' she retorted, rather brusquely.

The *paella* was brought in a large shallow metal pan and set on the end of the table. The yellow rice, coloured with saffron, glistened in the sunlight. Half a dozen prawns were arranged round the edge of the dish and there were chunks of chicken and possibly rabbit half hidden in the rice.

'I'll serve it, shall I?' said Cam, and he performed this task as expertly as a Spanish waiter.

As was customary in small Spanish restaurants, the plates had not been heated, so they concentrated on eating and did not talk. Fortunately the *paella* in the pan stayed hot. They both had second helpings and Cam finished up what was left.

'Mmm...very good,' he said, patting his flat midriff in a gesture of appreciation. 'Why does food always taste better out of doors, I wonder?'

Considering that he had probably eaten at some of the world's best restaurants, Liz felt his comments owed more to politeness than truth.

A car arrived and parked near hers under the pine trees. Two middle-aged couples got out and came to the table next to the one where Cam and Liz were sitting. The newcomers greeted them in Spanish, then continued their conversation in a language she didn't recognise and thought must be something Scandinavian.

The already large and still expanding expatriate community included many nationalities from all parts of Europe and also from North America. There had also been an influx of people from North Africa and South America, but they were mostly to be seen working on the land or selling goods in the street markets and *rastros*. Some were illegal immigrants, striving to make a better life for themselves. Many of the comfortably off expats disapproved of them, but Liz felt sorry for anyone forced, by poverty, to uproot themselves from their homelands.

'Shall we go for a stroll and have our fruit and coffee a little later?' Cam suggested.

'Won't the *señora* mind if we walk off without paying? Perhaps I should pay her first?'

'She won't mind if I explain. She's not a worrier like you are,' he said, before going inside the building.

Am I a worrier? Liz wondered. If I am, why does he want me in his life instead of some carefree butterfly like Fiona?

Cam reappeared. 'Let's go that way.' He indicated a rough track on the opposite side of the road passing the restaurant.

'You didn't pay her yourself, did you?' asked Liz, prepared to be angry if he had.

'You said you wanted to pick up the bill today.'

'Yes, but I know what men are. They like to be in charge.'

'Sometimes...not always,' he said mildly. 'There's a hawk.' He pointed at a bird hovering in the bright air.

They walked as far as a small deserted stone building that might once have been a dwelling in the time when all the terraces in this area were still under cultivation.

'It's hard for us to imagine spending our whole lives, from birth to death, in one small corner of the world,' said Cam, as they looked through what had once been the doorway to a single room. 'I don't think I could have stood it...day after day, year after year of relentless labour to scrape a living. I'd have had to go off and find out what was on the other side of the sierra—' waving his arm at the mountainside looming above them. 'But perhaps, having seen it, I would have come back and settled. There's a peacefulness here that you never find in a city or even a town.'

He turned to her. 'You've gone very quiet. What are you thinking about?'

'About your bombshell, of course. What else would I be thinking of?'

He came to where she was standing, putting his hands lightly on her shoulders.

'"Bombshell" implies something unpleasant. I can understand you being surprised, if you took me for a dedicated loner. But is the idea of being my wife so completely unacceptable that you can't believe I've suggested it?'

Then, before she could form her reply, he bent his head and kissed her mouth.

It was the lightest and most fleeting of kisses but, in an instant, it reactivated the feelings she had experienced in his garden after their first lunch together. Powerful sensations surged through her. In that moment she recognised the truth that her brain had been trying to deny. She had fallen in love with him.

As if that were not enough to cope with, Cam took his hands from her shoulders, but not to leave her free to step back if she wanted to. Instead he slipped his arms round her, gathered her close and kissed her again, this time with less restraint.

*   *   *

Some immeasurable time later—it might have been seconds or minutes, she only knew it was too brief to satisfy her body and far too long for her peace of mind—he brought the kiss to an end.

Still holding her, he said, 'I liked that. How about you?'

Stumped for a suitable answer, Liz freed herself. 'I think we should go back.'

It amazed her that her voice was steady when the rest of her felt like jelly. With a single kiss he had made her want him so badly that she couldn't believe the strength of the urges aroused in her.

'Whatever you say. It's your party.' He gestured for her to go ahead of him.

In a daze of conflicting emotions, she set out along the path.

Following her, Cam was pretty sure he knew what was going on in her mind. The kiss had made her understand what she hadn't taken in before: that her physical needs hadn't atrophied in the years she had been on her own but had merely been dormant and were now back in action and clamouring for satisfaction.

He noticed she was treading on stones that she would have avoided if she had been concentrating on the path instead of thinking about, and probably regretting, her response to his kiss.

Deliberately, he had not turned up the heat as high as it could have gone if he hadn't kept control. It would take time and patience to get her to the point when she wouldn't feel uneasy about the attraction between them.

He looked at her narrow waist and the feminine shape of her backside and he wished he could take her home and go to bed with her. But he was not going to do that—not today, not yet. It was too soon. She wasn't ready. He would have to be patient.

Back at the restaurant, they finished their meal with fresh fruit and coffee before driving back to Valdecarrasca. On the way, Cam suggested a detour to a *planterista* as he wanted some pots of geraniums for the sill of his street-side kitchen window.

'I thought geraniums needed sun, but there's a house near the bakery where they seem to thrive on a north-facing window ledge,' he said.

'Perhaps the owner has a sunny patio and swops them around,' said Liz.

He was the tallest, broadest passenger she had ever had in her small car and she was uneasily conscious of the long hard thighs on the other side of the gearstick and the rock-like chest that, not long ago, she had felt against her breasts.

'Perhaps.'

He had pushed the passenger seat as far back as it would go so that his backrest was several inches further back than hers. She knew he was watching her.

She forced herself to concentrate on driving, keeping an eye out for cars that, visible half a mile downhill, might vanish behind a bend just before the point when they met.

'Do you like driving?' Cam asked.

'I like country driving, but even that can be scary occasionally. I passed a van the other day whose driver was holding a mobile in one hand and making gestures with the other. He was on a straight stretch of road, but even so...'

'Maniac!' was Cam's comment. After a pause, he added, 'It makes a nice change to be driven...lets me look at the scenery in a way I can't at the wheel.'

The *planterista* they stopped at was not well-organised and some of the plants and shrubs on sale were in less than first-class condition. Cam decided to look for geraniums at one of the larger establishments catering to the thousands of villa-owners in the coastal belt.

'We could do that tomorrow,' he suggested, as they returned to the car. 'Also I wouldn't mind looking round the shops in Gata. I've been asked to a house-warming and I need to find a suitable present.'

Gata de Gorgos was a small town that straddled the main coast road and was famous for its cane furniture and basketwork shops. As well as going to the cinema there, Liz had browsed in the shops. She would have liked to go again, but she felt it was wiser to say, 'I really need to work tomorrow.'

'And you're still in shock and want time to recover...yes?'

She knew without glancing at him that there would be the hint of a smile at the corners of his mouth.

'Yes, that too,' she admitted.

The car was not locked and he opened the driver's door for her. 'OK, I'll give you a breathing space. How about going to Gata on Friday? I really would be glad of your advice on this house-warming gift...and we do need to spend more time together to help you come to a decision.'

'All right...Friday,' she agreed.

Next morning she had a call from Leonora Dryden.

'Liz, do you have an hour to spare this afternoon? I'd like to make a start on the portrait.'

At three o'clock, taking the party dress in a carrier, Liz walked round to the Drydens' house to be met by Leonora wearing one of her husband's cast-off shirts and a pair of paint-stained cotton trousers.

'It's good of you to come at short notice.' Leonora took her upstairs to her bedroom where Liz changed into the dress.

For the first half an hour of the sitting they chatted about general subjects until, suddenly, the older woman said, 'There's tension about you that wasn't there the other night. Is there something on your mind today?'

Liz hesitated and then, on impulse, said, 'Yes, there is, but I didn't know it showed.'

Leonora, who had been looking from her subject to the canvas at fifteen-second intervals ever since, satisfied with the pose, she had started work, now gave her sitter a longer look.

'Is it something you can discuss? A problem shared is a problem halved, as the saying goes.'

Again Liz hesitated before deciding to confide her dilemma. 'Cam has asked me to marry him.'

Much to her surprise, Leonora showed no sign of being startled by this information.

'I could see he was very taken with you at the party. I discussed it with Todd afterwards. He thought I was being over-imaginative, but men are less sensitive to nuances than women. But he did agree it was high time Cam took a wife and that you seemed an ideal person to take on that role. Why are you hesitating? Because you haven't known him long?'

'That's one of the reasons,' said Liz. 'How long did you and Todd know each other before you decided to marry?'

'We've known each other since we were children, so although we married very young it wasn't as rash a step for me as it would have been for most girls of twenty. Generally speaking I think women need to be twenty-five and men around thirty before they're sufficiently mature to commit themselves to a lifelong partnership. You and Cam know who you are and what you want from life.'

'He does...but I'm not sure that I do...except that I'd like to have children. But is that a good enough reason to marry someone?'

'Does Cam want children?'

'He says so.'

Leonora lapsed into a thoughtful silence. Eventually, she said, 'The question you have to ask yourself is, How will this man enhance my life and how can I enhance his? The feminists would have my guts for garters if they heard me but, generally speaking, I think being a wife—given that one's husband isn't a brute or a slob—is always preferable to being single. Men are so useful. If I didn't have Todd, I should have to read the bank statements and paint the seats in the garden and recharge the car's battery when, occasionally, it goes flat. I could do all those things if I had to, but I'd rather not, just as Todd doesn't want to be bothered with Christmas cards and duty letters to distant relations and choosing the fabric for new slipcovers.'

'But surely a marriage should be more than a matter of mutual convenience?' said Liz.

'Absolutely—but the day-to-day practicalities are an important part of life so it's crucial to be sure that you see eye to eye on the mundane matters. An obsessively neat person is unlikely to be happy with an untidy partner, and so on. Given roughly the same sort of personal habits, the next thing to consider is mind-sets. A free-thinker is never going to get along with someone extremely conventional. Todd and I have vigorous arguments on all sorts of topics, but in the important areas we're pretty much in agreement.'

'What do you see as the important areas?' Liz asked.

'Money, religion, politics and sex. Neither of us is extravagant, but nor are we mean. We're both atheists, but enjoy church architecture and music. We're both apolitical—despising all politicians impartially. We both take the view that fidelity is one of the keystones of marriage and affairs on the side are strictly off-limits. Have you discussed those areas with Cam?'

'Not yet. There hasn't been time to discuss anything much.'

Leonora took two steps backward and studied her canvas through narrowed eyes. 'I'd recommend thrashing them out as soon as possible. Cam's not the sort of man who will mind if you ask him point-blank what he thinks. What's more he'll tell you the truth and not just what he thinks you want to hear. He has one of the best-organised minds of anyone I know. There are not many subjects he doesn't have a point of view on.'

It was clear that she meant this comment to be encouraging, but Liz found it daunting, knowing that her own mind was far from well organised and there were lots of subjects about which she knew too little to have any firm opinions.

'I think that's enough for today. Time for a cup of tea,' said Leonora. 'I'll make it while you are changing. Would you mind leaving the dress here? I'd like to study that lovely shimmery effect.'

*   *   *

When Liz returned to her house, she opened her front door to find a bunch of flowers wrapped in florist's paper on the table inside it. There was only one person who could have left them there. Cam must have called while she was out and used the key she had given him to unlock the door.

Swathed in stiff dark green paper, the bunch of pale pink roses, cream carnations and various types of greenery that she didn't know the name of had a small envelope attached to it. Inside was a card on which he had written—

Thank you for yesterday.
Looking forward to tomorrow. C

Liz took the flowers to the kitchen. The only thing she had to put them in was a earthenware wine jug that was too rustic for the sophisticated flowers. As she snipped the tapes holding the stalks together, she wondered how much the flowers had cost. Probably a lot more than the price of yesterday's lunch. The envelope bore the name and address of the *floristería*. It was not the shop in the next village up the valley, but a florist in one of the coastal resorts. She wondered what other errand had taken him there. He would not have gone all that way just to buy flowers for her.

When the flowers were arranged, she went upstairs and sent him an e-mail.

Cam—I found your flowers when I got home from the first portrait session with Leonora. They are gorgeous. How kind of you—Liz

All evening she mulled over Leonora's advice. She had half expected the older woman to ask her about her marriage and wondered why she hadn't. Not that Liz would have wanted to talk about it. The past was better left undisturbed.

When, soon after ten, they set out for Gata, there were still long streamers of mist lying over parts of the valley, waiting to be dispersed by the sun. Most of the village streets were still in shade, and the people they saw were warmly wrapped up. One woman, returning from the *panadería* with bread in a cotton bag with *pan* embroidered on it, was wearing a quilted dressing gown, a garment often seen about the village during the morning.

Guessing that it might be cold inside the shops in Gata, Liz had taken the precaution of wearing a quilted gilet over a sweater over a shirt.

'What sort of house are you looking for a present for?' she asked, as they left the outskirts of the village.

'A converted farmhouse about ten miles further inland. It should be habitable by Easter, possibly sooner. As soon as it is, they'll be throwing a party. I suspect they'll be inundated with stuff they don't really want and I don't want to add to the junk.'

'Ornaments are the worst things to give,' said Liz, remembering a couple of horrors among her wedding presents. 'Not that you would, but some people can't believe that what they think is beautiful might be seen as hideous by someone else.'

She was looking at him as she spoke. When he laughed, it deepened the line down his cheek and gave her a momentary glimpse of his teeth. She had never thought of teeth as being sexy, but his were. Seeing them made her insides turn over. His hands had a similar effect. Out of the corner of her eye she watched the easy way he changed gear and his light handling of the wheel. Yet she had the feeling that, should an emergency occur, his reaction would be instantaneous and exactly right for the circumstances.

There were two ways to get to Gata and he chose the back road that followed the meandering course of a dry riverbed. Ahead, in the distance, they could see the massive outline of the mountain she had driven over with Deborah. Presently, a bend in the road opened the view of the impressive modern viaduct carrying the coastal *autopista* that Cam had mentioned when he was driving her to Alicante.

How incredulous she would have been, then, if someone had suggested that, within a few weeks, he would ask her to marry him.

As this seemed a good opportunity to broach the subjects Leonora had mentioned yesterday, she said, 'I read an article somewhere that said people contemplating marriage should make sure their minds are in tune on four subjects.'

'Which are?'

'Money, religion, politics…and sex.' She hesitated slightly before adding the fourth subject, the most difficult one for her to discuss with him.

'Having eye-witnessed some of worst excesses committed in the name of religion and politics, I don't have much time for zealots or politicians,' he answered. 'If the world is ever going to be a peaceful place, it will probably be the result of scientists finding ways to correct genetic problems. I'm very excited by the latest research into the human genome. I think that's where our best hopes lie.'

'That's exactly my view.' During a sleepless night she had worked out where she stood on three of the issues raised by Leonora.

'Good…then no problems there. Where do you stand on money?'

'As I've never had much, I don't really stand anywhere. I don't like people who are stingy, but I'm certainly not a member of the "buy now, pay later" brigade.'

'How do you feel about pre-nuptial settlements?'

'I don't approve of them *at all*,' she said, with vehement emphasis. 'But then I don't see the point of getting married if you think it might not be permanent.'

'But sometimes, despite both parties' good intentions, it isn't permanent and there are children to be provided for.'

'The moral of that is not to have children by a man unless you are certain he will stand by his obligations,' Liz said briskly.

'That's an idealist's view…sounds good in theory but often doesn't work out in practice.'

'I know…but I still think a pre-nuptial agreement makes it clear that there's no real love or trust in the marriage, that it's actually a cold-hearted exchange of assets, usually youth and beauty for fame and fortune.'

'You're thinking of showbiz alliances, I imagine. Like anyone who works in front of the TV cameras, I have a small amount of fame and some modest assets in a trust that was set up by my grandparents when I was a small boy. They were more prudent than my parents who are both incurably extravagant. Is your mother comfortably off?'

'She has a nice bungalow and enough to live on. I don't have to help her,' said Liz, in case he had been wondering whether her mother would be a liability he would have to shoulder. 'But I don't think my mother and yours would have anything in common. My background is very ordinary.'

'Are you an inverted snob, Liz?' He gave her a quizzical glance. 'One thing that any journalist learns early on is that a person's worth has nothing to do with their place in the pecking order. I once spent time with a man who cleaned London's sewers. In all the ways that really matter, he was a far better person than a man with a seat on several boards whom I interviewed shortly afterwards.'

'So he may have been, but that isn't to say they would have been comfortable in each other's company,' she pointed out.

'Possibly not. Although if they had been holed up together in some tricky situation they'd have probably got along fine...with the sewer man taking command and the boardroom guy glad to let him, I shouldn't wonder. But that's beside the point. All that matters in our case is that you and I are on the same wavelength. Whether our family members like each other is their problem, not ours.'

By this time they were on the outskirts of Gata. The streets behind the main thoroughfare had been built when traffic consisted of mule-drawn carts and Cam needed to give his full attention to passing lines of closely parked cars and turning tight corners.

He was able to find a parking spot not far from the main through road and soon they were in one of the many shops selling cane and bas-ketware and glass and pottery. Here, and in other shops they visited, there was usually a middle-aged or elderly woman who emerged from the rear of the premises to keep an eye on them. When they found Cam spoke fluent Spanish, they seemed glad to gossip with him while Liz roamed the aisles between the crowded displays.

It was in the fourth shop that she noticed a set of sturdy wine goblets made from glass with a greenish tinge and bubbles of air in the stems that she thought would be perfect for the house he had described. Cam agreed with her and bought twenty of them and two matching jugs.

While they were being wrapped in newspaper and packed in a carton, Liz saw a square glass vase that was perfect for the flowers he had given her.

As he stowed their shopping in the back to the car, Cam said, 'Time for coffee...if you don't mind having it in a bar. I don't think Gata runs to anything smarter.'

'A bar is fine by me.'

On days out with Deborah, she had been into places they wouldn't have used back in England but found acceptable here, where small-town and village bars were mainly men's places, lacking the refinements of cafés and tea rooms designed to suit a feminine clientele.

The first bar they came to was empty apart from the barman who was sweeping up the litter of sugar wrappers and cigarette ends on the floor beneath the bar stools. The television was on and two fruit machines were flashing their lights, but the noise level wasn't intolerable as it sometimes could be in bars.

Liz chose a table away from the fruit machines and watched Cam's back view as he leaned against the bar while the man behind it dealt with his order. If she had needed any confirmation of her feelings about him, this moment would have been proof. Because he was with her, she would rather be here, in this scruffy Spanish bar, than anywhere on earth.

He carried two cups of coffee to the plastic-imitating-wood table with its ashtray, plastic pot of toothpicks and plastic container for the squares of paper napkin that, in Liz's experience, were never very absorbent.

'Not the most glamorous ambience, I'm afraid,' he said dryly, before turning away to fetch two glasses of white wine.

'You're used to more glamorous places than I am,' said Liz, when he came back.

'Sometimes...not always.' He pulled out a chair and sat down. 'Anyway it's the company that counts.' He smiled at her.

If only it counted for him as much as it did for her, she thought, with a pang. If only there was a chance that he might come to love her.

Cam drank some coffee. 'Now, where had we got to with your list of things to discuss? We've done religion and politics. As far as money is concerned, my view is that when people marry they should pool their resources, allocate themselves some spending money and confer about all their other expenses. Does that seems sensible?'

'Perfectly,' Liz agreed, aware that her pulse-rate had quickened with anticipated nervousness.

'Right, so that leaves only one more item on the agenda,' said Cam. 'But perhaps the most key of them all.' He paused, and there was a gleam in the steel-grey eyes that made her pulse beat even faster. 'Sex. What aspects of it are we supposed to discuss?'

CHAPTER SIX

Donde no hay amor, no hay dolor

Where there is no love, there is no pain

'I THINK fidelity is the big issue. I know I couldn't cope with an ''open'' marriage. But is fidelity possible for someone like yourself who's been used to...to variety?'

'Not only possible, but preferable. It was asking someone to marry me when I was a nomad, and there was always a chance I wouldn't come back, that was impossible.'

'But don't you think you might get bored with only one partner? A lot of men do.'

'A lot of men have unsatisfactory sex lives. They don't understand women's needs so they don't get the response they need and start looking elsewhere. They don't realise the problem lies with them.'

She wanted to ask, How come *you* understand? But this wasn't a subject she was comfortable with. Her unease was a hangover from her childhood when sex had never been discussed. Even when her father was not present, her mother had dealt with Liz's questions awkwardly, making her realise that, if she wanted satisfactory answers, she would have to find another source of information.

In the end, most of what she had learnt had come from books and magazines. But knowing the theory and putting it into practice were two different things, she had discovered.

From the other side of the table Cam watched Liz apparently studying the imitation wood grain of the tabletop. There was a slight frown between her eyebrows. He guessed that she wasn't seeing the pattern on the plastic but had retreated into a private part of her mind which he might never penetrate.

He said quietly, 'If you decide to marry me, I will be faithful to you. That's a promise. I'm not in favour of open marriages either.'

She looked up at him. He could read the uncertainty verging on disbelief in her eyes and he cursed the fact that, the first time they met, he had had Fiona with him. Obviously meeting one of his former girlfriends had confirmed all the gossip Liz had picked up about him. If she hadn't met Fiona, she might have taken it less seriously.

'My grandmother used to quote a saying about reformed rakes making the best husbands,' he told her. 'You wouldn't expect me, at my age, not to have had any relationships, would you?'

'No...but it does sound as if you've had rather a lot of them.'

It wasn't often that he found himself lost for words. Words were his stock in trade. But explaining his past life to Liz was a great deal harder than explaining the complexities of the Middle East or African politics to several million television viewers.

'You must have seen films or read about World War Two,' he said. 'When men didn't know if they were going to come back from their next bombing mission, or their next Atlantic convoy, they grabbed life with both hands while they had the chance. Women did too, even in those days when normal codes of behaviour were a great deal stricter than they are now.'

She nodded, listening intently.

'Reporters who cover war zones tend to feel the same way,' he went on. 'It's a high-risk occupation so they live for the present. Tomorrow may never happen. But now, unless I'm very unlucky, I can expect to live as long as my grandparents did. I can plan for the future.' He reached across the table and put his hand over hers. 'I'm hoping to spend it with you...raising a family and enjoying life together.'

He had hoped that she might react by turning her hand palm upwards and curling her fingers round his. But her hand remained motionless.

She said, 'Nowadays most people have a trial run before they marry. Don't you think that might be wiser than rushing into matrimony straight away?'

'Did you have a trial run with your husband?'

As he had noticed before, any mention of her husband lit a flicker of pain in her eyes.

Liz knew it was natural for Cam to be curious about her marriage and perhaps, one day, she would tell him the whole story, but not now, not yet.

She shook her head. 'Our families were very conventional. We both lived at home till we married. A trial run wasn't an option. I was never a rebel and neither was Duncan.'

'What was his job?'

'He was an accountant with an insurance company.' To Cam, she felt sure, such an occupation would seem the nadir of dullness.

'Was it what he wanted to do?'

'He wasn't unhappy doing it. I think he accepted that most people don't find their work exciting. Somebody has to do the dull jobs. He did enjoy his hobby—coin-collecting. He belonged to several collectors' clubs and wrote articles on numismatics.' That probably made Duncan sound even duller, she thought.

Rather to her surprise, Cam said, 'That's a fascinating field. I know next to nothing about it, but I can understand its appeal. My grandfather collected stamps but he didn't attempt to interest me in them. He believed that a passion for collecting couldn't be instilled but had to spring up naturally. However, getting back to the question of trial runs, I think, in a village like this, there's no point in inviting critical comment. In London and New York, no one gives a damn what anyone does. But here they have different values.'

Liz had no doubt he was right as far as the older women were concerned. Most of them would have been virgin brides. But, according to what Alicia had told her, Spanish girls were rapidly catching up with their peers in northern Europe, even to the extent of setting up house with their boyfriends.

Alicia had also confided that, for her own generation, sexual relations ended with the menopause—and a good thing too, she had added, suggesting that her own experience of physical love had been a tiresome duty rather than the delight it was supposed to be.

In her still far from fluent Spanish, Liz had ventured to ask what their husbands thought about that. Alicia had shrugged her plump shoulders, at the same time pulling down the corners of her mouth and rolling her eyes. 'Men are men and will find their pleasures where they can,' she had said dismissively.

Deborah, when Liz had relayed this comment to her, had said, 'Haven't you noticed the ''clubs'' all along the main coast road? Club is a euphemism for brothel. I expect that's where they go. Don't look so shocked. Men are like that. If your husband wasn't, you were lucky.'

And, in that respect, she had been, Liz knew. There was no doubt in her mind that Duncan had always been faithful to her. He had disapproved of promiscuity and avoided colleagues who went boozing together or played the field. He would not have got on with Cam. They were poles apart.

Cam had withdrawn his hand and was drinking his wine and watching her with a faintly amused expression.

'It's not so long since you were warning me not to step out of line. Now you're the one suggesting we go to bed together, and you haven't made the decision to marry me yet—or have you?'

She felt herself flushing. 'No, I haven't. I still think the idea is mad.'

'On the contrary...eminently sane. But we won't argue about it. Bring me up to date with your online life.'

They didn't get back to the village until late afternoon, after looking round some more of Gata's shops and then having a late lunch during which Cam steered the conversation away from personal matters and made Liz laugh more often than she could ever remember laughing at a meal table.

When he dropped her outside her house, he got out to open the boot and give her the vase she had bought.

'Thank you for lunch,' she said, as he handed it over.

'Thank you for being my shopping adviser. Are you going to Benissa tomorrow?'

Benissa was a cathedral town where, on Saturdays, a picturesque street market supplied Spaniards, expats and tourists with excellent produce.

'Probably.'

'Why don't we go together and free a car parking space for someone else to use?'

Against her better judgement, she said, 'All right. What time?'

'Is half past nine too early?'

'No, that would be fine.'

'Hasta mañana.' Seeing that a heavy lorry was coming down the narrow street and would not be able to pass his car, he quickly returned to the wheel.

Presently, as she was rearranging his flowers in the new vase, Liz knew it would have been wiser to avoid his company for a few days and give herself time to think more clearly than she could when she was with him.

That evening, intending to do some work, she could not resist looking at the photo of him she had saved from the TV channel website. By using a photographic program, she was able to enlarge it and print it on a small colour printer she had bought at a special offer price. When used with special paper that was more expensive than ordinary paper, the printer produced prints of a quality as good as regular photographs.

Later, lying in bed, she spent a long time studying every detail of Cam's physiognomy, from the way his hair sprang from his broad, high forehead in an almost straight line with the hint of a peak in the centre, to the exact shape of his incisors.

She found that, if she covered his left eye with her hand, the right eye looked curiously stern. When she covered his right eye, the left had the sexy glint that she found so disturbing. With both eyes exposed it was less noticeable, as was the sternness.

She got out of bed for a hand mirror and studied her own eyes. Their expression seemed identical. Perhaps a difference was only noticeable in a photograph, but the only portrait photograph she had was in her passport and it was too small to be studied in the same way.

What worried her was that she remembered studying a picture of Duncan in just this way when she was in her late teens. Was she any wiser than she had been then? Older, yes—but not necessarily any more sensible.

She remembered some lines read at school. *Friendship is a disinterested commerce between equals; love, an abject intercourse between tyrants and slaves.*

Duncan, mildest of men, had not been a tyrant. Nevertheless her marriage had been a kind of slavery, a bondage from which there had seemed to be no escape until, suddenly, she was free—and sick with shame because the price of her freedom had been his life.

At midnight, unable to sleep, she went up to the flat roof for the first time since the night Cam had brought Fiona to La Higuera and she had seen them embracing by the guest room window.

Now the only room alight was the sitting room, but its occupant wasn't visible. Perhaps he was sitting on the sofa that had its back to the windows. If the television had been on, she would have seen the blue glow of its screen. But it wasn't so he must be reading.

At least they had that in common. They were both insatiable readers. But was it enough to build a marriage on?

Benissa market was already bustling when they arrived at the street where it took place. On either side was a row of terraced houses, some tall, some smaller, but all with black-painted iron *rejas* protecting the ground-floor windows, narrow balconies at the windows above, and black or well-polished brass knockers on the doors. Each terrace had a narrow pavement and a roadway. One road was at a slightly lower level than the other and between them was a narrow railinged garden with palm trees towering above shrubs and daisy bushes.

Today the two roadways were occupied by stalls displaying piles of shiny purple aubergines, ruby-red and dark green peppers, garlic, mushrooms, strawberries, artichokes, oranges and many other fruit and vegetables. Crowding the fronts of the stalls were local housewives, some pulling shopping trolleys and others with small dummy-sucking children in pushchairs. The air was loud with voices, most of them speaking Valenciano, the language of the region. But foreigners speaking German, Dutch, French, English and various Scandinavian languages added to the babel. Several children were eating *churros* from a stall at one end of the market, and a teenage girl was managing to navigate through the crowd on Rollerblades.

Many curious and interested glances were directed at Cam, Liz noticed, for not only was he taller than most of the shoppers, but he had the air of being someone special. She wondered if he would be recognised, though this was not the kind of place where people would expect to find someone well-known on TV. Despite its superior climate, the Costa Blanca had never had the once fashionable and now somewhat disreputable image of the Costa del Sol in the south of Spain.

'These *piel de sapo* melons are good—if you like melon,' she said, picking up one shaped like a rugby ball, its name deriving from the fact that the green rind with darker blotches did resemble the skin of a toad.

Cam bought one and insisted on putting them both in the rucksack he had slung over one broad shoulder. Though the local people were always well-mannered, once or twice, on previous visits to the market, Liz had been jostled or elbowed aside by the kind of foreigner who felt he or she had the right to be served before other shoppers.

With Cam beside her, she knew this would not happen. His presence was like a shield. She felt an atavistic pleasure in being with someone larger and stronger who, in the unlikely event of an affray breaking out, would see it as his duty to protect her. Being a man's equal was good in many ways, but there were still circumstances in which any sensible woman would welcome a strong male arm around her, or a tough masculine body stepping in front of her to ward off whatever the threat was.

Just as she was thinking this, Cam, now standing behind her, leaned forward to pick out a grapefruit, the movement bringing his chest into contact with the back of her shoulder. At the same time she caught an aroma of soap, or shaving cream, or shower gel, that was more subtle than the fragrance of aftershave.

In that instant she knew that, however misguided it might be, she was going to accept his proposal of marriage. She was as incapable of resisting her feelings for him as she had been helpless to resist her girlish love for Duncan. All she could do was pray that, this time, it would turn out differently.

'Sorry, am I crowding you?' said Cam, looking down at the same moment that she looked up at him.

'Everyone's crowding everyone,' Liz said, with attempted lightness. But her heart was thudding against her ribs and her voice came out husky instead of cool. How was it possible to feel these intensely private and personal sensations in such a public place?

Still holding the grapefruit out towards the stall-holder, Cam bent his head towards hers. In a low voice, speaking close to her ear, he said, 'But these well-padded *amas de casa* and *hausfraus* don't have the same effect on me that you do. I'm controlling a strong desire to kiss you.'

She repressed an impulse to say, Why don't you? knowing he wasn't a man to resist a challenge, however inappropriate the setting.

Before she could think of another answer, his teasing expression changed and he said quietly, 'You've made up your mind, haven't you?'

His discernment stunned her. How could he read her mind so quickly and clearly? It was only moments since she had made the decision.

Then the stall-holder took the grapefruit from his hand and asked, *'Algo más, señor?'*

'Nada mas.' Cam handed over some coins and was given change. Turning to Liz, he said, 'Why don't I take our shopping back to the car

while you have a browse round the other street? I'll join you there and then we'll go for a coffee.'

Taking her assent for granted, he took charge of the plastic carrier she was holding and turned away.

She watched him till he disappeared from view, and then she made her way slowly to a street at right angles to the market, where clothing and shoes were sold. There were also stalls selling cheap watches and jewellery or colourful rugs. The vendors of these were usually Africans or North Africans, their ebony or lighter brown skins adding a cosmopolitan touch to the small town atmosphere.

Usually Liz enjoyed browsing, but today her mind was focused on the shift about to take place in her relationship with Cam. Only yesterday she had told him a marriage between them was madness and now, as soon as he came back, she would have to admit she was ready to go ahead. Not only ready but eager—although she wouldn't tell him that.

When Cam rejoined her she was watching, with a couple of small children, a wind-up toy frog swimming around in a blue plastic bowl.

'Hi,' he said, putting a hand on her shoulder. 'If you'd like one of those for your bath, I'm in a spending mood.' Before she could stop him, he had asked the stall-holder, in Spanish, to wrap one up for her.

'Cam, you're crazy,' she protested.

'No, just happy,' he answered, smiling. 'How would it be if we put a jacuzzi in the courtyard and took outdoor tubs...you and me and the frog? I saw one advertised in the *Costa Blanca News*, or it may have been that freebie paper the *Entertainer*.'

'A jacuzzi would ruin the courtyard. It would be an eyesore. How can you even suggest such a thing?'

'For the pleasure of seeing you look horrified.' He presented her with the frog, now wrapped in gift paper. 'He's a place-holder until I can enjoy the privilege of sharing your bath.'

Place-holder was a computing term she had already explained to him. She said, 'You don't know for sure that I've decided to marry you. You're only assuming that.'

'Am I wrong?'

'No,' she admitted.

'Then let's find a secluded corner and start making plans.' He took her free hand in his and led the way through the crowd.

The bar most popular with the expats who shopped in Benissa was on the main square, near the fountain. But it was a noisy establishment where the tables often had to be shared. Cam took her to a quieter place where they could sit by themselves.

Having ordered coffee and *cava*, he said, 'I bought something else in the market. Another place-holder.' He felt in his trouser pocket and brought out something wrapped in coloured tissue paper fastened with sticky tape.

'A place-holder for what?' she asked, as he handed it to her.

'For something I need to discuss with you.'

Normally Liz was a person who unwrapped parcels carefully, patiently unfastening knots and trying not to tear the paper. This time she unwrapped the package quickly and, when she saw what was in it, gave a gasp of surprise.

Apart from the frog, the only thing in the market that had caught her eye for more than a moment had been an inexpensive bracelet of transparent blue and green beads. It was the sort of thing that looked pretty on the suntanned wrist of a teenage girl but she had felt was too young for her. It seemed extraordinary that Cam should have spotted the one thing she had liked.

He took it and put it on for her. 'It's a place-holder for an engagement ring. I don't know what kind of jewellery you like so we'll need to choose that together. Meanwhile you can wear this nonsense.' He lifted her hand to his lips and brushed a kiss on her knuckles. 'And that is also a place-holder until we can seal our bond in the traditional way.'

At this point the bar waiter brought their coffee, two glasses of champagne and some little dishes of nibbles. He released her hand and leaned back in his chair. But, as the waiter arranged the things on the table, Liz was aware that Cam was continuing to watch her.

She put her hands in her lap and looked down at the delicate web of beads. They were the colour of sea water.

'To us,' said Cam, raising his glass.

'To us,' she echoed. 'But, Cam, I don't need an engagement ring. I'm perfectly happy with this pretty bracelet.'

For a second or two, he frowned. Then the hint of displeasure vanished and he said easily, 'As you wish. How soon can we be married? From my point of view, the sooner the better. I'd prefer the quietest possible civil marriage. But you may have other ideas.'

'No, that would suit me too. I expect we can find out what the formalities are on the Web. But won't your parents expect to be present?'

'They may expect to be invited but I don't particularly want them there. Had my grandparents been alive, that would have been different.' He paused. 'I'm not suggesting you shouldn't invite your mother if you would like to have her there.'

'I couldn't invite her without asking my aunt and she'd want my cousins included. I think it would be much better not to have anyone. I can always put the blame on you. They'll be too excited at having you in the family to stay in a huff for long,' said Liz.

'We had better fix a trip to the UK and break the news in person to both our families,' he said. 'What I particularly want to avoid is any press coverage. As far as I'm concerned my private life is private.'

'My friend Deborah takes *Hola!*, the Spanish version of *Hello*, and I admit to reading the copies she passes on, but I wouldn't want to be in it, however huge a fee was offered me.'

'Good, because there is no possibility that La Higuera will ever be featured in it,' said Cam. 'Working on the assumption that you were going to say yes, I was thinking last night that— unless you want to sell your house and invest the capital—it might be a good idea to have a door in the wall connecting the two courtyards and use your house as a visitors' cottage. That way you could use one of the present guest bedrooms as your studio and the other one, hopefully, we shall need as a nursery.'

'Cam, what if I can't give you children? Have you considered that possibility?'

'Having children is always the luck of the draw. If we can't, we can't,' he said shrugging.

'But children are one of your reasons for getting married,' she reminded him. 'When people are in love it's different. If their plans go awry, they have their love to fall back on. Ours is a practical marriage…a matter of mutual convenience.'

'And that means that, unlike couples who marry with their heads in a cloud of illusion, we aren't expecting perfection. If it doesn't pan out exactly as we hope, we'll adjust to that more easily than people who feel they're entitled to everything life has to offer. Maybe my experiences in Africa and other third world countries have made me overly impatient with some aspects of first world culture. I haven't a lot of time for the woman so obsessed with her right to motherhood that she spends thousands of pounds trying to get pregnant—money that would spare hundreds of African women the drudgery of walking miles to fetch water, or restore the sight of thousands of blind people in India.'

It was the first time Liz had heard this note of passionate intensity in his voice.

'I think it's hard for a man to understand how deeply some women long for children,' she answered. 'I wouldn't go to those lengths myself. Like you, I feel that if getting pregnant doesn't happen easily, then one should just accept it and get on with other things. But it has to be said,' she added, 'that a lot of people would be more supportive of the kinds of good causes you've mentioned if they didn't have an uneasy feeling that their donations were being siphoned off by corrupt officials rather than benefiting the people they would like to help.'

'I'm afraid you're right about that...and, from what I've seen, their fears are often justified. It's a mad world we live in...which is all the more reason for establishing our own pocket of sanity. We have a lifetime to discuss and argue the serious issues. Today let's just enjoy ourselves. To celebrate, I thought we'd drive into the mountains and have lunch at a hotel that I'm told has a spectacular view. We can drop off our shopping on the way through Valdecarrasca.'

As they drove back to the village, Liz was conscious of a huge sense of relief that her indecision was over and the die was cast.

'Rather than going to both houses, let's put all the stuff in my fridge and you can retrieve yours when we come back,' Cam suggested.

'OK…whatever you say.'

He gave her a smiling glance. 'I wonder if you'll say that to all my suggestions? Somehow I suspect not.'

'You don't want a doormat wife, do you?'

'Absolutely not. But when we cross swords, I'd rather we did it in private, not like some couples I know who fire broadsides at each other across other people's dinner tables.'

'I've known people like that too. It's always horribly embarrassing for the onlookers. Hopefully we won't need to cross swords.'

'I think we're bound to occasionally. No two people ever see eye to eye on everything.'

While he unloaded their shopping, Liz pulled down the passenger's sun-screen and found, as she had expected, that it had a mirror attached to it. Quickly she retouched her lipstick, remembering what he had said, at the market, about wanting to kiss her. When *would* he kiss her? she wondered. Perhaps this afternoon, when they returned from their outing.

She remembered his previous kisses and their effect on her. Even the memory set up a tremor inside her. She forced herself to think about something else.

They had left the village behind them and were driving west towards the far end of the valley and the more isolated valleys beyond it when Cam said, 'Do you mind if I play some music?'

'Not at all.' She wondered what kind of music he liked to listen to while driving. Her guess would be classical orchestral stuff, or jazz.

Moments later, to her complete surprise, she recognised the voice of Michael Crawford singing 'The Music of the Night' from *Phantom of the Opera*. This was followed by the beautiful duet 'All I Ask of You', a song that expressed her deepest beliefs about the nature of love.

Liz leaned her head against the backrest, closed her eyes and let Crawford's magical tenor and the equally lovely soprano voice of his leading lady sweep her away into a romantic dreamworld.

As usual, the tender lyrics brought a lump to her throat and the prickle of tears to her eyes.

Expecting to have the rest of the disc to recover herself, she was startled when, as the last notes of the song died away, there was a click and she felt the brakes being applied.

Opening eyes that were bright with emotion, she saw they were now on a straight stretch of road where stopping would not impede any other vehicles that might come along.

'Liz, I'm sorry if that music brings back painful memories. It's one of my favourite shows and I should have realised you probably saw it with your husband.'

'Actually I didn't. I saw it with a girlfriend,' she said, blinking, her voice husky.

'But you're upset,' he said, frowning.

'Not for the reason you thought. I'm afraid I'm just a sucker for schmaltz,' she admitted.

'Are you? I wouldn't have guessed it.'

'It's not something people advertise. Please...do play the rest. It's one of my favourite shows too.'

'All right...if you're sure.'

She smiled at him. 'I'm sure.'

Although it was not yet the height of the almond blossom season and some trees still had bare branches, in the more sheltered folds of the foothills there were almond groves where all the trees had their branches clustered with white and pink blossoms. The pink flowers came in two shades, one darker than the other. Here and there, bends in the road brought orange groves into view, the bright fruit hanging among the glossy dark foliage like baubles on Christmas trees. Always, when Liz saw oranges growing, her spirits lifted and she felt privileged to be here instead of trapped in the rat race.

The hotel that was their destination was built close to the crest of a hill, not far from a deep ravine and facing towards the distant coastal plain. The main building was faced with stone to blend into the landscape and all around it had been planted the thyme and lavender that thrived in this type of terrain.

They had a drink in the bar before being shown to their table in a dining room with many brick-edged arches.

'This area is supposed to have been the last stronghold of the Moors, who fought to stay here after the decree expelling them,' said Cam, as they waited for their first course. 'One can imagine how they felt. They had been in Spain for seven hundred years. They'd worked miracles making it fertile, and suddenly—out!' He made a sweeping gesture with his hand.

They discussed the expulsion of the Jews and Moors, who had done so much to enrich Spain's culture, through most of lunch. Liz enjoyed the meal, but Cam was critical of the food and the service.

'I make allowances for the shortcomings of small country restaurants,' he said. 'But this place is setting out to be first class and has to be judged by more exacting standards. We won't be coming here for our honeymoon.'

She had not thought that far ahead, but evidently he had.

'We'll have to pick out a *parador*...unless you would rather we spent the time outside

Spain. If there's somewhere you'd like to go, you have only to say so.'

Guessing that travelling abroad would be no treat for him, she said, 'A *parador* sounds fine to me. Have you stayed at a lot of them?'

'Only three. The modern one by the sea in Jávea, the one near the top of the Sierra Nevada, which is also modern and mostly used by skiers, and one in the restored castle at Tortosa on the river Ebro. I stayed there with my grandparents when they drove me back to school in England after a summer holiday with them. There are plenty of others to choose from.'

When they left the hotel, Liz assumed they would go home the way they had come. But Cam said there was another route he wanted to show her. It turned out to be a narrow byroad, with many twists and turns, and views that were some of the loveliest she had ever seen. Here, in wilder country than they had passed through on the way, the slopes surrounding the road were bright with yellow gorse.

'Could we stop for a minute?' she asked. For, though Cam was driving very slowly, she longed to get out and gaze at the colours and shapes of the mountains on the far side of the valley.

He stopped the car and they got out and stood at the edge of the track in companionable silence.

'I wish I'd brought the camera,' she said. 'I'd love to have a shot of this on my website…though I think it would take a professional photographer to do it justice.'

When Cam didn't answer, she glanced at him. He was standing with folded arms. As she looked at him, he unfolded them and beckoned her to him with both hands.

Her insides leaping about like a parcel of frogs, Liz moved towards him. A yard away she stopped.

'I think it's time I kissed you,' he said.

'You already have.'

'But in different circumstances. Now we are an item, as they say.'

He reached out and, placing his hands on the sides of her waist, drew her closer until there were only inches between them. Liz put her hands on his chest, feeling its warmth and solidity against her palms.

She wanted to say, I love you, but knew that she couldn't. Love, unless it was mutual, could only be a burden to the person who did not feel the same way. All she could do was to close her eyes and tilt her face up to him.

The touch of his lips sent the frogs into a frenzy. He gathered her into his arms and held her possessively close, his mouth persuading hers to open.

The kiss might have gone on indefinitely but for the sound of a tractor on the track above them. Cam did not let her go, but he lifted his head and relaxed his hold so that, though still embraced, they were no longer locked together when the tractor driver came by and shouted a greeting above the noise of the motor.

As the tractor trundled downhill, Cam said, 'If this were a hot afternoon in England, we could find a grassy spot and make love in the sun. But in Spain the ground doesn't lend itself to such pleasures.'

By 'making love' did he mean kissing, or more? she wondered. Had he changed his mind about not going to bed with her until they were married?

'Let's move on,' said Cam, keeping his right arm round her until he had opened the passenger door.

At the bottom of the hill they had to rumble and bounce over a dry riverbed and then up a short stony slope that brought them back to a road. On the way back he played the lovely 'Concierto de Aranjuez', a concerto for guitar and orchestra by the famous Spanish composer Joaquin Rodrigo.

She had heard part of the concerto on her first visit to Spain and later discovered the romantic story behind it. Rodrigo, who had died at the age of ninety-seven in 1999, had been seriously ill with diphtheria as a child of three. It had left him almost totally blind, but he had trained as a musician and, aided by Braille and his Turkish wife, also a professional musician, had become a successful composer, his most famous work— the one they were listening to now—being known all over the world

Back in Valdecarrasca, Cam didn't drive to his house as she'd expected but stopped the car outside hers. 'I'll bring your stuff down in a few minutes,' he said.

Liz wondered if that meant he was planning to stay with her for the rest of the day and where that might lead. Was she ready for it? For more kisses, yes. But the rest...? She wasn't sure.

It was half an hour before Cam reappeared with her shopping.

'Sorry to keep you waiting. As I was unlocking the door, the phone started ringing. I've only just got off the line.'

Although she was still very nervous of what he might have in mind—the effect of the wine with lunch had long since worn off—she felt she had to offer him a cup of tea.

'Tea would be great.'

'Was your phone call something interesting?' she asked, thinking it might have to do with his work.

'Not very. It was from a guy who needs a shrink to sort out his problems but doesn't want to pay the fees so he unloads them on me. He's his own worst enemy, and a bore, but I don't like to be too short with him. We go back a long way. Do you have girlfriends like that?'

'I knew one unloader in London, but we aren't in touch any more. What used to irritate me was that she talked for hours about her life but never showed the smallest interest in mine. Not that I had anything to unload—' or nothing that I would talk about, was her thought '—but I think, if I had, she would have switched off.'

'Most people are pretty self-centred,' said Cam. 'From a journalist's point of view, that's good. On a personal level it's a turn-off.'

At her suggestion, they had tea on her flat roof. As they chatted and had second cups, there was nothing in the least amorous in his manner. She began to think she had panicked unnecessarily. Well, not panicked precisely, she corrected herself. But she had been in more of a flap than most women of thirty-six confronted with the possibility that, before the day was out, they might find themselves in bed with a highly desirable man whom they loved and were going to marry.

In England alone, not counting the rest of the world, there must be thousands of thirty-something singletons who would count themselves lucky to have sex with someone like Cam—even without marriage being on the agenda.

It was just that—

Cam interrupted her train of thought. 'What I must get down to, before long, is some intensive work on the stuff for my website.'

He discussed some more thoughts he had had since their last conversation on the subject. Then he rose from his deckchair. 'No time like the present. I'll go and do some work now. Let me carry this down—' replacing his cup on the tray. 'You stay here and relax.'

On impulse, Liz said, 'After a large lunch, we won't need much supper. Would you like to come back about seven and share a pomegranate salad?'

'Sounds good. See you later.' He picked up the tray and went down the outside staircase, leaving Liz to wonder if she needed her brains tested.

Wouldn't any man, invited to supper, assume that it was an invitation to stay the night?

CHAPTER SEVEN

Amor, tos y dinero llevan cencerro

Love, a cough and money cannot be kept secret

LIZ stayed on the roof for some time after he had gone. She had only to close her eyes to be back among the golden gorse of the mountain-side with Cam's strong arms around her and her lips parting under his. She could remember the taste of his mouth, the pleasant male smell of his skin and the warm rock-like feel of his shoulders as she slid her hands higher. Before the tractor came by, she had been on the point of slipping her arms round his neck.

The memory of those moments made her long to repeat the experience. If only it could stop at kisses...hours of rapturous kissing that was an end in itself without leading on to...

Her mind flinched from thoughts she did not want to recall. If only she could be certain that this time it would be different.

From the window of his workroom Cam saw her stand up, take a long look round at the sunlit vineyards, and then go slowly down the stairs.

She would never know how difficult it had been for him to force their conversation into a businesslike channel that would give him a pretext for leaving instead of staying on the roof and resuming the embrace interrupted by the tractor.

Surrounded by a waist-high wall, the roof was not totally private, although a sunbather lying on cushions on the tiled floor would not be seen. But the chances of anyone observing them, had he kissed her, were slight. It had not been that possibility that had restrained him—their relationship was probably the subject of speculation already—but rather an instinctive sense that making love to Liz was not going to be as straightforward and uncomplicated as his previous relationships with women.

For one thing it was four years since she had made love. For another she had only been to bed with one person in her life. And thirdly she was not in love with him which normally, for a woman like Liz, would be essential before she could let her hair down.

All told, getting it right was going to be extremely tricky. Getting it wrong disastrous.

He had no experience of women who were not experienced. Or of women who had been through the trauma of shock and grief she had suffered. He wanted her; had wanted her for some time. But, if they were going to spend the rest of their lives together, it was important, at this stage, to keep his own feelings under control and put her needs before his.

Whether he would be able to do that tonight was an open question. She was beginning to arouse him merely by smiling at him, or crossing her long slim legs, or making some gesture with her hand that made him want to reach out and catch it and hold it against him. Which, of course, would immediately undo all his efforts to make her relax with him. There was a chasteness about her that he found both refreshing and exciting.

He remembered a conversation with his grandmother relating to her favourite musical *My Fair Lady*. She had been at the opening night of the original stage production in 1956. At the end of her life she had taken her mind off her illness by replaying the video of the film version. More than once Cam had watched it with her, and the line that had prompted their subsequent conversation was Professor Higgins's complaint, 'Why can't a woman be more like a man?'

'The trouble is that nowadays girls *are* more like men,' his grandmother had said, with a sigh. 'Too much like them, in my view. Young men have always sown wild oats, but I don't think girls should.' She had been worried about one of her great-nieces who, not yet twenty, had already had several affairs.

When Cam had pointed out that sowing wild oats could not be done without female co-operation, Mrs Fielding, her perspective typical of her age group, had replied, 'They should do it with older women, not the sort of girls they might marry.'

Despite her out-of-date views, Cam had been influenced by his grandmother. Apart from anything else, she and his grandfather had embodied the kind of lasting happiness that was a universal ideal.

In many ways, Liz reminded Cam of his grandmother. He knew they would have liked each other. What his parents would make of Liz he couldn't tell. Not that their opinion mattered to him, but it might matter to her if she sensed they were hostile.

While Cam was thinking about her, Liz was relaxing in a scented bath. At least her body was relaxed and she was attempting, not altogether successfully, to think calming thoughts.

After her bath she did her nails and then used an expensive revitalising facial mask her aunt had given her at Christmas. These were things she usually did every Sunday but they helped to fill the time until seven.

It was a few minutes past the hour when she heard the rap of the knocker and went to let Cam in. He had changed into pale whipcord trousers and a cotton shirt finely checked in navy and white with a navy sweater slung round his shoulders, the sleeves casually tied across his chest.

'Hi.' He greeted her with a light kiss on the cheek. 'You look very nice.'

'Thank you.' Because there was a significant drop in the temperature after dark, she had lit the fire and put on a long dark brown wool skirt—the colour of black chocolate—and a short-waisted clingy sweater of lambswool mixed with angora in pale blue.

'What would you like to drink? Wine…gin…beer?' She gestured for him to take the large wing chair by the fire that, like most of the furniture, she had bought from Beatrice Maybury.

'Wine, please…red if you have it.'

Guessing he would like red wine to drink with their meal, she had already opened a bottle. He was still on his feet, looking at the print she had hung on the chimneybreast, when she brought him a glass. He remained standing until she sat down.

'How do you cope with the firewood problem?'

'You mean when it's dumped in a pile in the street and has to be carried through the house to the back yard? Mrs Maybury didn't mention that…and I didn't think to ask her. I'd never lived in a house with no rear access before.' Liz laughed. '*Caveat emptor*…let the buyer beware. I guess I was lucky that was the only hidden snag. It could have been something much worse. It's hard work getting the wood through, but a two thousand kilo load lasts me a long time.'

'You won't have to do it any more,' he reminded her. 'When we're married, I'll be stacking the logs and laying the fires.'

'I assumed you paid someone to do the stacking for you.'

He shook his head. 'It's a job I enjoy. There's something satisfying about a well-stacked log store, and it's good exercise. I like laying fires too. There's an art in it.'

'It seems an unlikely art for you to practise.'

'There's a streak of the boy scout in most men. Not that I ever was a scout. Were you a guide?'

'No, I went to dancing classes run by a retired chorus girl. In her teens my mother had dreamed of becoming a dancer. She projected that frustrated ambition onto me. She wanted me to be picked for the school's troupe who danced at charity shows. But, to her disappointment, I wasn't. I quite liked tap, but I wasn't much good at it.'

'Can you remember the steps? Give me a demo.'

Liz hesitated. Then she got up, lifted her skirt to mid-calf and, on a patch of tiled floor between the rugs, did a short routine she remembered and sometimes danced in the kitchen while waiting for the kettle to boil.

'I'd like to see you do that in black fishnet tights,' said Cam. 'Can you do high kicks and splits?'

'I could when I was twelve. I shouldn't care to risk it now. I might do myself an injury,' she said, laughing and letting down her skirt. 'Excuse me a minute. I need to put something in the oven.'

'I thought we were only going to have some fruit salad,' he said, as she turned towards the kitchen.

'We are, but I thought a small hot starter might be a good idea. It won't take long.'

When she came back she asked him to help her move a small table, that normally lived against the wall that blocked off the staircase, to a position in the centre of the room.

Without being asked, Cam fetched the two upright chairs from where they stood when not in use. With two other chairs from upstairs, Liz could seat four people for dinner.

She had everything ready on a tray in the kitchen. It didn't take long to lay the table.

'Right: if you'll sit there, I'll bring in the starter,' she said, hoping he wasn't expecting anything spectacular.

She had to use oven mitts to handle the earthenware dish from the oven. 'This is a poor man's version of angels-on-horseback,' she explained, setting it in front of him.

'I like anything wrapped in hot bacon. What have you used instead of oysters?'

'Pieces of banana…and I've also done anchovies on toast with a dab of alioli on them.'

Considering how many top-class restaurants he must have dined at, Cam was gratifyingly enthusiastic about her efforts. He couldn't have been nicer had he been in love with her, she thought. But that was wishful thinking and she must not indulge in it.

It was important to keep her feet firmly on the ground and remind herself at regular intervals that it was only good manners, not affection, that made him such an agreeable companion.

The fruit salad did look rather special. She had mixed some strawberries and Chinese gooseberries with the glistening red seeds from the pomegranate and, in place of cream, she served *queso fresco*, the Spanish equivalent of *fromage frais*.

'Did you know that the pomegranate is the symbol of Spain?' she asked, while she was serving it. 'A crowned pomegranate was Catherine of Aragon's personal badge.'

'How did you find that out?'

'When I was studying historical needlework at college. Stylised pomegranates appear on all sorts of period textiles. There are pomegranates in that copy of Elizabethan blackwork that I worked for one of my exams. But most people wouldn't recognise them as such.'

Cam rose from the table and went to look at the framed piece of embroidery she had indicated. When he came back, he said, 'You're a woman of many parts...tap dancer...expert embroiderer...what else am I going to discover about you?'

A sudden shiver of apprehension ran through her. What if she turned out to be a disaster in bed? What if, despite the excitement induced by his kisses, there came a point when...?

'Not nearly as many discoveries as I'm going to make about you, I expect,' she said, trying to sound carefree. 'Your life has been far more exciting than mine. I've never been outside Europe.'

'That reminds me, after supper why don't we take a look at the Spanish Tourist Board website and pick out a *parador* for our honeymoon?' he suggested. 'By the way, I've looked into the question of our getting married in Spain and I don't think it's going to be possible. There are no facilities for civil weddings at any of the British consulates. They suggest going down to Gibraltar as an alternative. But I think it would be easier to do it in London by special licence.'

'Might the fact that I'm now a Spanish resident be a complication, do you think?'

'Possibly. I'll check. Up to now, I've never been here long enough to become a resident. That's something else I must look into.'

Unlike Cam, Liz did not have a dishwasher. After supper, he insisted on washing up for her. Then they took their coffee and what was left of the wine upstairs to her workroom.

From force of habit she had left her bedroom door open. As she mounted the stairs ahead of him, she wondered what construction Cam would put on the sight of her double bed with its old-fashioned white cotton quilt and brass head and foot rails. Might he think she had left the door wide open deliberately?

The last time they had sat side by side at a computer she had felt uneasy and made an excuse to move away. This time she was still intensely aware of his nearness, but there was no way to avoid it. Nor, to be honest, did she want to.

'Try keying in *parador* dot, e for España, s for Spain,' Cam suggested, when she was online.

His guesswork proved correct. A moment later they were at the Paradores Website, where a map marked the locations of more than eighty *paradores*.

'I'll show you the ones I've stayed at.' Cam put his hand over hers where it rested on the mouse and moved the cursor to a point near the north-east coast. Without removing his hand, he said, 'Click there.'

The feel of his palm on the back of her hand did crazy things to her pulse-rate. 'Why don't we change places and you do the clicking?' she suggested.

'I like it the way we are. Don't you?'

She could tell by the tone of his voice he was looking at her, not the screen, and that he was smiling.

Then he put his free hand on her shoulder, the one farthest from him, and moved the tips of his fingers over the softness of her sweater. 'This looks and feels very strokable.'

'We're supposed to be doing a tour of the *paradores*,' Liz said, her voice suddenly hoarse.

'I'd rather be doing a tour of you,' he said softly, and his hand moved down her back and moved slowly round her midriff till it lay over her ribs just below her left breast.

She stopped breathing. Or that was how it felt. As if she had gone into freeze mode, the way a computer sometimes did when its circuits became overloaded. The strange thing was that although all her normal responses had suddenly ceased to operate, others, normally dormant, were behaving like Geiger counters reacting to radiation.

There was nothing she could do but wait, staring blindly at the screen, for whatever was going to happen next. What happened was that Cam bent towards her and kissed the part of her neck just under her ear while, at the same time, his hand moved upwards to caress her breast.

'Mmm…your skin smells delicious,' he murmured, as his right hand stopped covering hers and came up to cradle her cheek and turn her face towards his.

There were moments, while he was kissing her mouth and gently fondling her breast, when Liz thought she could not contain the feelings he aroused, that he would be sure to guess the sensations he was inducing. But then, when the tension had built to the point when it had become almost unbearable, he took his mouth and his hand away.

'You're right...this won't do,' he said. 'If we're going to reserve these pleasures for our honeymoon, we had better get on with deciding where to spend it...and the sooner the better, don't you think?'

Later, when they were downstairs, saying goodnight, Liz had a wild impulse to say, Don't go. Stay with me tonight.

If he had kissed her, she might have done. But instead he bent over her hand in the most formal way, as if they were barely acquainted, not two people planning to marry.

After he had gone, knowing that she couldn't sleep, she got ready for bed but then went back to the computer and retraced the route they had followed. Jarandella de la Vera...Sigüenza... Ciudad Rodrigo...Chinchon...all of them well worth a visit but none, in Cam's view, the perfect place to start married life.

To her it was immaterial where they went. All she could think about was their wedding night and how it might turn out.

Tonight's experience should have allayed her misgivings. As it had...until she remembered that long, long ago she had felt similar sensations. Kissing and touching was one thing. Full intercourse was another. Just because she had come close to ecstasy tonight did not mean she could take it for granted that all would be well when he finally took her to bed.

They flew to England from Valencia, an airport that, unlike Alicante, was not seething with expats and holidaymakers but catered mainly to Spaniards, most of them well-dressed people flying around Europe on business.

They also flew business class which to Liz, used to the cramped conditions in economy, was unaccustomed luxury. Also, she soon discovered, travelling with Cam was like travelling with a prince. Even when he wasn't recognised, there was something about him that made people helpful and deferential. As his companion, she shared this special treatment.

At Heathrow, a driver was waiting to take them to Cam's apartment in central London where, that evening, his close family were coming to a dinner party organised by a catering firm he had used before.

Cam's flat was in a block overlooking the Thames and the view of the river from the large living room made it seem less citified than she had expected it to be.

'On my grandfather's advice, I bought a place to live as soon as I could afford to apply for a mortgage,' he told her, while showing her round. 'The way property prices have risen in London—or any big city—it hasn't been difficult to keep upgrading, especially for a bachelor without any of the usual family overheads. If you like the flat, we'll keep it. If you don't, we'll find somewhere else.'

He opened the door of a comfortable twin-bedded room. 'You'll be in here for the time being. My room overlooks the river and the third bedroom is an office with a sofa-bed for when my sisters and their children make use of the flat. I told them there wouldn't be room for them here tonight.'

'Won't they think that strange? I mean usually…'

'…people about to be married share a room,' he finished for her. 'Our sleeping arrangements are no one else's business, and after three or four hours of their company you'll be glad to see the back of them. Other people's relations can be heavy going, though I think you'll find Miranda on your wavelength. I have some phone calls to make and you'll want to get unpacked.'

Left on her own in his guest room, Liz surveyed her surroundings. The decor had the hallmarks of a professional designer's work and, though tasteful, lacked the personal feel of his house in Spain. She guessed that he didn't regard this place as a home so much as a necessary pied-à-terre and an investment.

A little while later Cam knocked on the door. When she opened it, he said, 'I have to go out for about an hour. The catering people won't show up much before seven. But in case you should be in the bath, or having a nap, I'll tell the hall porter to let them in. See you later.'

He didn't kiss her goodbye as a normal husband-to-be would have done, she noticed. Since the night he had come to supper, his behaviour towards her had been as circumspect as if they were living in a more conventional era. Was that because the waiting time was putting a strain on his will-power? Or was there some other reason?

It crossed her mind that he might have arranged to visit one of his former girlfriends with a view to releasing the controls he was exerting in his relationship with Liz. For a moment the thought made her steam with anger. Then she forced herself to dismiss it. If she thought Cam capable of that sort of behaviour, what was she doing committing her future to him?

*   *   *

Liz didn't emerge from her room till half an hour before the guests were due to arrive. She was wearing the dress she had worn to the Drydens' party, but with her hair in a French pleat instead of loose.

Cam was nowhere to be seen, but the catering team was in action. A long table, probably a board on trestles concealed by a long cloth, had been set up and laid for twelve. A lot of well-organised activity was taking place in the kitchen. Sophisticated flower arrangements that had not been there earlier had been placed around the living room.

'Would you like some champagne, madam?' asked one of the caterers, coming out of the kitchen. She was wearing a discreet little black dress and looked in her early twenties.

The 'madam' made Liz feel ancient. 'Yes, thank you, I would.'

She had taken her first sip when Cam appeared. He was wearing a dark grey suit with a lighter grey shirt and mimosa-coloured silk tie. His hair was damp from the shower as it had been the first time they met.

His gaze swept over her. 'Do you think a market bracelet is right for that dress?' he asked, raising an eyebrow.

She looked at the beads encircling her left wrist. 'I think it's perfect.' Something impelled her to add, 'Far more romantic than diamonds.'

'Diamonds are for queens or trophy wives. I think these are more your style.' He took from his pocket a long slim leather-covered box containing a string of stones that gleamed like crystallised sea water. Taking the bracelet from its satin bed, he put the box aside and came towards her.

'Hold this a moment while I take that thing off.' Having removed the beads, he tossed them into a nearby wastepaper basket. Then he took the aquamarines from her and fastened the clasp and safety clasp.

'Thank you. It's beautiful,' said Liz. 'But I still want to keep the beads. They were your first present to me. We might at least go through the motions of being a normal couple, don't you think?' She went to look in the basket, which was empty apart from the Spanish bracelet. 'I'll put this in my room.'

As she walked away from him, the doorbell rang.

She disliked his mother on sight, and she thought it was probably mutual. Mrs Nightingale, as she was now, was a tall woman with a discontented mouth and critical eyes.

'We have been *most* curious to meet you,' she said, as they shook hands after Cam had introduced them. 'Cameron has eluded matrimony for so long, we thought he would never settle down. I hope you know what you're letting yourself in for. Journalists make even worse husbands than diplomats. You will never enjoy any sense of permanence.'

To her own surprise, Liz found herself smiling. 'But I shall never be bored which I think is much more important,' she said cheerfully.

Mr Fielding was more tactful than his former wife. He congratulated his son and was complimentary to Liz but, again, she could see hardly any family resemblance except that he too was tall. Clearly most of Cam's genes had skipped a generation and came from his grandparents.

When, later, they sat down to dinner, she realised his seating plan was carefully thought out. He had placed his parents at opposite ends of the table with their new partners beside them. He and Liz sat opposite each other in the centre of the table, she flanked by two of his brothers-in-law and he by two of his sisters, with his third sister next to their mother and a brother-in-law next to his father. So Liz was two places removed from her formidable mother-in-law and within easy speaking distance of Miranda, the sister closest to him in age and temperament.

Even so, the feeling of being scrutinised by so many strangers made it a stressful occasion. And although Cam gave a masterly imitation of a man who has found the perfect woman for him, he could not deceive her.

It was long past midnight before Miranda and her husband were the last to leave.

'I expect you are thankful that's over,' said Cam, when he came back from seeing them into their taxi, as he had with all his departing guests.

'Not at all. They were charming to me,' she said, not entirely truthfully, 'and the dinner was delicious.'

'Yes, the food was excellent,' he agreed. 'Now I think we had better turn in. Tomorrow it's my turn for ordeal-by-in-law. Off you go. I'll put the lights out.' He gave her a chaste kiss on the cheek and then moved away to start switching off the room's many linen-shaded lamps.

When she was in bed, Liz tried to continue reading the second-hand book she had bought for the journey. But the story failed to stop her doing a mental postmortem on the evening, and then thinking about Cam and the reasons why they were sleeping apart in a world where other people hopped into bed together within hours of meeting.

She wondered what would happen if she went to his room and told him she couldn't sleep. But she knew she didn't have the courage to do that, much as she longed to end the suspense of waiting for their wedding night.

In his bedroom, Cam, who hadn't worn pyjamas since he left school, was sitting up in bed with the duvet drawn up to his waist and his laptop resting on his thighs.

He was reading an article in a bi-monthly magazine whose print edition was distributed to more than thirty thousand senior business executives in the US. The purpose of the publication was to explore business methods in a world transformed by technology, and to suggest ways to profit from the new business landscape.

The magazine's website was one he visited regularly, but tonight it failed to hold his attention and he soon moved on to another of his sources of information. He was reading a piece about the so-called gender wars when he came to a sentence relating to women and fundamental values of twenty-first-century western society.

'If you live in a distillery, maybe non-alcoholic lager is an exciting and refreshing sensation,' the columnist, a man, had written.

The analogy reminded Cam of some thoughts he had had a few days ago about why Liz appealed to him and why, when he wasn't actually fighting down arousal, he was glad that she didn't have a long line of lovers in her past or the brash sexual confidence that characterised many of today's women.

It was typical of her that she had retrieved the cheap bracelet from the wastepaper basket and insisted on keeping it, and equally typical that she had chosen to wear it tonight despite its unsuitability with her expensive dress.

'We might at least go through the motions of being a normal couple, don't you think?'

There had been a sparkle of anger in her eyes that had made him want to grab her and kiss the daylights out of her. But with his family due to show up at any second, it hadn't been the moment to wreck her lipstick and give himself a hard-on.

Even thinking about holding her could do that to him. She was like the mysterious and exciting parcels his grandparents had put under the tree when he spent Christmas with them; parcels he could hardly wait to unwrap. But none of them had contained anything he wanted as much as he wanted Liz.

The only fly in the ointment was that for her it was going to be a second wedding and a second honeymoon. Inevitably, everything was going to remind her of the first time and the husband she had loved with all her heart and probably still did.

'Sleep well?' Cam asked, rising, when Liz went to the kitchen and found him having breakfast.

'Yes, thank you,' she lied. 'Did you?'

'Always do. Would you like tea or coffee?'

'Tea, please…but there's no need for you to disturb yourself. I can deal with it. I'm sorry I overslept. You should have banged on my door.'

'I thought a lie-in would do you good. How about some scrambled eggs? They're my speciality.'

'Can I try them another time? As we're going out to lunch, toast and marmalade will be enough for me.'

Sharing a breakfast table with Cam for the first time, she remembered the hundreds of breakfasts she had cooked for Duncan who had eaten them in silence, reading a tabloid newspaper popular with Middle England. They had never talked much at meals. They had never talked much, period, she thought regretfully.

Cam kept up an easy flow of conversation about the news and feature stories he had read in the online editions of the broadsheets before he got up. He had printed out an obituary notice of a famous embroiderer that he thought would interest her.

'That was kind of you,' she said, as he handed the stapled pages to her.

'My pleasure.'

Even at this early hour, his smile activated butterflies in her stomach.

It wasn't until they were ready to leave for the suburbs that she discovered he had brought with him from Spain two expensive presentation boxes of *turrón*, the sugary confection made at Jijona, in the province where they lived, and eaten at all times of year but especially at Christmas.

'You told me your mother and aunt both had a sweet tooth,' he reminded her.

'But I didn't expect you to remember it.'

'I want them to warm to me. I ordered some flowers as well. The hall porter has them. We'll pick them up on our way down to the garage.'

Liz hadn't realised the block had an underground garage and Cam kept a car in it. She had assumed that in London he used taxis or chauffeur-driven cars like the one that had met them yesterday.

When she said as much, he said, 'Did you think I never went into the country...never stayed with friends in other parts of England?'

'I suppose I thought you were almost always abroad.'

'I was…but there were gaps when I managed to get to the weddings and christenings of friends who took to matrimony and domesticity long before I did. I should be a godfather many times over if my views hadn't disqualified me.'

Liz knew that it was a flaw in her character to be embarrassed by the kitsch ornaments her father had bought for her parents' garden, and the style of the net curtains her mother had chosen for the bungalow's two bay windows. Even the ornamental name plate hanging on chains from the roof of the porch, and the name itself, made her uncomfortable. She despised herself for the feeling, but she couldn't help it.

He had scarcely parked the car before the front door opened and her mother and aunt surged down the path to meet them, a mixture of excitement and shyness visible in their faces.

The lunch, at a hotel, a few miles away, that Cam had organised by e-mail was more relaxed and enjoyable than Liz would have believed possible. It made her realise what an extraordinary gift he had for getting on with people and drawing them out.

It was in the middle of the main course, when apéritifs in the bar and white wine with the potted shrimps starter had already brought a flush to the two ladies' powdered cheeks, that he said, 'Mrs Bailey...or may I call you Maureen and Sue?'—with a smiling glance at her sister.

'Of course you can, dear.' As the endearment slipped out, Mrs Bailey looked uncertain for a second, then laughed and patted his hand which was resting on the table. 'It won't be long before we're all family, will it? Have you set the date yet? June is a lovely month for weddings.'

'That's what I wanted to talk to you about. We'd like to get married very quickly and quietly by special licence. The problem is that if we ask you and Sue, we shall have to ask members of my family. That's something I want to avoid. We'd like it to be as private as possible. Later on we may give a big party for everyone we know. But I feel—and Liz agrees—that, at our age and in our circumstances, just the two of us and a couple of witnesses is the best way to do it. I know this may disappoint you. But I hope, when you've thought it over, you'll agree it's the right decision.'

The sisters looked at each other, disappointment writ large on their chubby faces. It looked to Liz as if, even in the short time since her last visit, they had both put on several pounds.

On impulse, she said, 'But we'd like to arrange a treat for you to make up for the disappointment. What we thought would be fun, while we're on our honeymoon, is for you two to spend a week at one of those swish health farms. You've always said you'd like to go, Mum, and this is your chance.'

She knew it would cost a lot and might empty her bank account, but she felt it would be worth it.

'Ooh…that would lovely, wouldn't it, Sue?' said her mother, her expression brightening.

It was just as well that Cam was more abstemious than his guests. By the end of the lunch, the sisters were as animated and giggly as Liz had ever seen them. She felt sure that Mrs Nightingale, had she been present, would have been horrified that her son was forging a relationship with people she would have found unacceptable.

It was after three when they left the hotel and returned to the bungalow.

'What about a nice cup of tea?' said Mrs Bailey.

'Why don't we let Liz and Sue take care of that? I'd like to see your back garden,' said Cam.

'He's a lovely bloke, Liz,' said her aunt, when they were alone in the kitchen. 'You're a very fortunate girl, my love. It's not easy for someone of your age to marry again. What a lucky thing you moved to Spain. Who would have thought there'd be someone as nice as Cam living next door?'

In the garden, Maureen was telling Cam about the prizes her neighbour had won at the local flower show.

'Was your son-in-law keen on gardening?'

'Duncan? No, not at all. Liz looked after their garden. Duncan's interests were coin-collecting and sport—football and cricket. Hours he spent watching matches. Liz didn't mind. She liked reading better than TV. Not like her mum. A telly addict, she calls me—' with a giggle. Then her face clouded. 'Such a tragedy…him being drowned like that. She was devastated, poor kid. We wouldn't have been surprised if she'd had a nervous breakdown. They'd meant the world to each other since they were in their teens. Never looked at anyone else, either of them. But that's all behind her now. You can't live in the past, especially not at her age.'

'No, you can't,' Cam agreed. 'I hope, when we get back from our honeymoon, you and Sue will come and stay with us.'

'We'd love that. I feel a bit guilty I've never been down to see Liz's house, but the fact is

I'm scared of flying. I know it's silly, but I am. But I've got to get over it.'

'Lots of people don't like flying. Someone you probably know by sight—' he named a well-known TV presenter '—has flown more than a million miles and still doesn't like it.'

'Really? I think he's lovely...he's one of my favourites.'

Looking out of the picture window at the rear of the lounge, Liz wondered what they were talking about.

Later, on the way back to the apartment, she asked him.

'Oh...this and that,' he said vaguely. 'I've invited them to stay with us in Spain. By the way, it was a brainwave on your part to suggest we send them off to a health farm to make up for not being present at the wedding.'

'There's absolutely no need for you to involve yourself, Cam. I can afford whatever it costs.'

'Those places are pretty expensive,' he said. 'I'd like to pay my share. What's mine is yours, and what's yours is mine. That's how I see our financial future. Do you disagree?'

'No...not in principle...but in practice it's going to be heavily weighted in my favour, your income being so much larger than mine.'

'Up to now, but not necessarily for ever. If your website business takes off and my career declines, you could find yourself supporting me,' he said, turning his head to smile at her.

On the morning of her wedding day, Liz was woken by the alarm she had set the night before. The register office ceremony was taking place early in order for them to fly to Madrid and then drive the rest of the way to the *parador* they had chosen for their honeymoon.

For a while she lay thinking about that other day, seventeen years ago, when there had been a billowing white taffeta bridal gown hanging on the front of her wardrobe, and a garland of white silk flowers for her hair on the dressing table. Her mother had wanted a big wedding, and Liz herself had not been averse to making the day as special as possible.

A tap at the door interrupted her thoughts.

'Come in.'

'Breakfast in bed for the bride,' said Cam, coming in with a tray. He was dressed in jeans and a tight white T-shirt that showed off his muscular build.

'Good morning. What luxury.' Liz sat up in bed. She was wearing an Indian cotton nightdress with white embroidery round the neck and down the front. A less modest garment was packed in her case for tonight.

The tray had a woven cane edge and short legs. He placed it across her lap.

'No last-minute doubts? No eleventh-hour jitters?' he asked, sitting down near her feet.

'Not for me. How about you?'

'I can't wait to call you my wife…and to make you my wife.'

The burning look, so early in the morning, startled her. He looked as if, for two pins, he would make love to her now.

While she stared at him, startled, he rose. 'I have things to do. See you later. *Buen provecho.*'

This was an expression the Spanish used before people started to eat. She had used it herself to the men who worked on the vines if she passed while they were sitting on a drystone wall, having a snack before continuing their labours.

When the door had closed behind him, Liz moved the tray and hopped out of bed to brush her teeth. To her surprise she had slept well.

My last night in a bed by myself, she thought: the same thought she had had on that other wedding morning. Except that then she had been impatient to surrender her virginity, eager to find out what it was all about, the mysterious act of union so often described but only fully understood by those who had experienced it.

Remembering her first experience, she did feel a moment of panic. Then she reminded herself that Duncan had also been a virgin and Cam was a man of experience who knew what he was about. At least she hoped he did.

He was not around when she took the tray to the kitchen and washed up the few things on it. Then she had a leisurely bath before starting to do her face. Her hair had been cut and blown dry yesterday morning. She was going to wear it loose.

Her wedding outfit was a cornflower-blue suit of classic design, the jacket buttoning high enough to be worn without a top under it. The colour emphasised her eyes and was also an excellent foil for the aquamarine bracelet. She had found a long chiffon scarf of exactly those two colours to twist round her neck with one end floating in front and the other behind.

She had finished dressing when she heard Cam speaking on the telephone in the living room and went to join him. Still in conversation, he looked her up and down. Was he disappointed? Had he expected something more high-key and glamorous?

'Thanks…goodbye.' He replaced the receiver and came towards her. 'You look beautiful. I was just about to bring these into you, but you don't have to wear them now if you'd rather keep them for later.'

He opened his closed hand, palm upwards, and she saw that he had been holding a pair of aquamarine earrings that matched the bracelet.

'They're lovely…but, Cam, I don't have anything for you.'

'You are giving me yourself. That's all I want.'

He said it with such unexpected tenderness that she felt a lump in her throat. 'Would you put them on for me, please?'

'Sure. Hold this.' He gave her one of the earrings and removed the butterfly fastening from the other. Deftly he threaded the pin through the tiny hole in her ear and fitted the fastening.

She hadn't realised the touch of his fingertips against the sensitive skin at the back of her lobes would send such a strong frisson through her.

When he had dealt with the other, he said softly, 'And tonight I will take them off for you.'

His voice held the promise of other intimacies that quickened her pulse and brought a flush to her cheeks. She wanted to say, I can't wait, but it was only half true.

It had gone so badly wrong before…not just once but many, many times. Would it go right this time? Or had part of the fault been hers? Was there something wrong with her?

Would tonight be a new beginning, or another disaster?

CHAPTER EIGHT

*Tanto es amar sin ser amado como responder
sin ser preguntado*

To love without being loved is like answering
without being asked

It was a two-hour drive from Madrid's airport at nearby Barajas to the thirteenth-century castle where they were going to stay.

'I'm glad to be back in Spain,' said Liz, when they had skirted the outskirts of the capital and the landscape was becoming increasingly rural. 'Even though this part of the country is different from our *provincia*, it still feels more like home than London. I don't mean I didn't enjoy staying at your apartment—'

'I know exactly what you mean,' Cam cut in. Like her, he was still in his wedding clothes but had removed his jacket, taken off his tie and unfastened the collar of his shirt.

'London is fine for short spells, but it isn't what I define as ''real life''. No big city is—at any rate not for me. I guess, at heart, I'm a country bumpkin.'

'Anyone less like a bumpkin is impossible to imagine,' Liz said, laughing. 'A grandee of Spain is what I should take you for, if you were a stranger. You look the way I imagine Spanish grandees...though the ones I've seen in the papers have been disappointingly short and ordinary-looking. The only one who came up to my expectations was the Duke who married the Infanta Elena...and even he isn't as good-looking as you are.'

He shot her an amused look. Then, the *autopista* being clear, he reached for her hand and lifted it to his lips. The car being left-hand drive, it was her left hand, the third finger now adorned by the beautiful and unusual combination engagement and wedding ring he had chosen for her. A wide band of matt gold set at intervals with lozenge-shaped sapphires and aquamarines, it looked modern but also reminiscent of the jewels worn by merchant princes' wives and mistresses during the Renaissance.

'Thank you, Mrs Fielding. I think you allow partiality to colour your judgement, but why not? It is our wedding day. If we don't see each other through rose-coloured glasses today, we're unlikely to do so in twenty years' time.' He returned her hand to her lap.

Although, on the flight, he had confined himself to a glass of champagne before lunch and another with it, Liz had drunk several glasses, which perhaps accounted for her outspokenness and her relaxed mood as the car Cam had rented cruised smoothly along the motorway taking them south.

But after they branched off the main highway, and once they were more than halfway to their destination, her misgivings kicked in again. Outwardly this trip had all the makings of an idyllic honeymoon. But, beneath the surface, the problem had not gone away. It was still there, like an anti-personnel mine embedded in a seemingly peaceful field. And like a mine it was capable, if detonated, of causing horrendous emotional damage from which their marriage might never recover.

When the *parador* came into view, it looked like an illustration in a fairy tale, a fortress built on the crest of a hill, its towers and battlements outlined against the blue sky. The approach road wound its way up by a series of hairpin bends until it bridged a ravine and they entered the castle by way of an arch and found themselves in a large courtyard now converted to the *parador's* car park.

'Not many people here,' said Cam, parking alongside a car with a 'D' badge indicating German ownership, and another with the Swiss

'CH' badge. 'But perhaps some people staying here have gone out for the day, and I expect there'll be night-stoppers turning up later.'

Their arrival must have been noticed by someone inside the castle. As he was unlocking the boot, a young man still in his teens came out to help with the luggage.

The interior of the castle had a baronial atmosphere combined with the *ambiente* of a luxurious hotel. Cam signed the register and handed over his passport. Then they were taken by lift to a higher floor, along a corridor and up a stone staircase to their suite.

This had a spacious lobby leading into a sitting room which in turn led into a bedroom, dominated by a massive four-poster bed, with a bathroom leading off it. While Cam was talking to the porter, her attention was caught by the views from the sitting room windows.

The suite, she realised, was in one of the castle's square towers with one window overlooking a formal Spanish garden and the other looking down on a large swimming-pool that shimmered invitingly in the afternoon sun.

'Great for cooling off in the summer, but too cold for comfort now, I should think,' said Cam, looking over her shoulder.

The porter had gone. They were alone.

'I've asked them to send up some tea. Meanwhile...'

He turned her to face him, took her face between his hands, and bent his head to kiss her, first on one side of her mouth, then on the other, and then with his lips matched to hers. But it was a gentle rather than passionate kiss and, after a moment he straightened to smile at her before pulling her into his arms and holding her close in a bear hug.

'This is one of life's perfect moments,' he said. 'The right place...the right person... nothing to do but relax and enjoy ourselves.' She felt him kissing her hair. Then he gave a soft laugh and added, 'But I suppose, being a woman, you want to unpack your case and get all those drop-dead outfits hung up.'

In fact Liz was disappointed when he slackened his hold. Her clothes were the last thing on her mind.

She leaned back in his arms and said, 'The new things I bought are all rather simple. I didn't expect there to be much dressing up.'

'The foreigners probably won't cut much of a dash, but if Spanish people from the nearest town come to eat here they will dress up. If they're spending money, they like to make an occasion of it. Whatever you wear will be right.

You have excellent taste. Come on: let's get our kit sorted, then we can really relax.'

'This bathroom is gorgeous,' said Liz, a few minutes later, when she was putting her toilet bag on the marble counter surrounding the twin basins.

He came to stand in the doorway and look at the peach and white decor she was admiring. Then a buzzer sounded and he went to answer it. Moments later, Liz heard a young female voice speaking Spanish and Cam replying. Somehow the language accentuated the sexiness of his voice.

She returned to the sitting room to find a plump girl in a black skirt and white blouse arranging tea things on the low table in front of the sofa. *'Buenas tardes, señora.'*

Liz smiled at her. *'Buenas tardes.'*

There were sandwiches and Spanish pastries to sustain them until the dining room opened at nine.

When the girl had gone, Cam said, 'The tea will be far too strong. Let's fish out some of the tea bags.' He extracted a couple from the pot.

They sat on the feather-cushioned sofa and had afternoon tea and discussed the appointments of the room until Cam said, 'It's a long time till dinner. Why don't we have a bath and then a *siesta*?'

By *siesta* did he mean a sleep? Liz wondered. Or the other kind of *siesta*?

'That sounds a good idea.'

'We can bath together. There's plenty of room. It's a large tub. I'll go and run the water.' He rose and disappeared.

A bath *together*! Liz remained where she was, paralysed with shyness. On her previous honeymoon, they had reached the hotel late, had dinner almost immediately and then gone for a walk along the promenade before going upstairs to their room. Everything had happened with the lights out. Now, all these years later, with her body no longer as taut as it had been at nineteen, she was going to have to climb into a tub with a man who, in terms of physical contact, was almost a stranger.

She heard the water starting to run and wondered if she ought to go into the bedroom and start undressing. The trouble was she had no idea how she was supposed to behave in this situation. It seemed best to sit tight and wait for Cam to call her or come for her.

The water seemed to run for a long time, but then, as he had said, it was an extra-large bath designed to accommodate Texans and Scandinavians and other men of Cam's height and build.

When he appeared in the doorway, he was naked except for a towel wrapped round his hips. Liz rose to her feet, trying to look less uncertain than she felt. They met at the halfway point between the sofa and the bedroom door. He took her hand in his and led her to the bathroom where he closed he door behind them. Then he started to undress her.

'I've been looking forward to this for a long time,' he told her, unfastening the buttons of her blue jacket. She had removed the scarf on the aeroplane.

Tongue-tied, she kept her eyes fixed on his hard brown chest. She had never in her life felt more self-conscious and awkward...or more tense. Her insides were in knots.

Cam opened the jacket and slipped it off her shoulders so that it slid down her arms. He hung it on one of the hooks on the back of the door, which was within his reach.

'This is pretty.' He was looking at her pale blue silk camisole edged and strapped with white satin.

He reached round behind her to unbutton the waistband of her skirt and pull down the zipper. He slid it down over her hips and let it drop to the floor so that she could step out of it. Then he picked it up and hung it with the jacket. The skirt being lined, this left Liz in her tights and panties. Quickly, she slipped off her shoes, reducing her height by two inches.

Though it seemly unlikely he knew the silk camisole was cut on the cross and therefore more elastic than straight-cut fabric, Cam took hold of the hem and drew it upwards so that she had to raise her arms to allow him to draw it over her head. She thought he would reach for the clip of her white embroidered net bra, but instead he put his fingers inside the waistband of her tights and drew them downwards over her hips and thighs. Then he put his hand behind her right knee and raised her leg in order to peel the nylon away from her calf and foot. Seconds later her tights were lying on the floor in a diaphanous swirl like the snake's sloughed-off skin she had seen on one of her rambles in the mountains.

Cam put his hands on either side of her bare waist, drew her towards him and gave her a lingering kiss. Now there was only the fragile texture of net between her breasts and his chest. Surely he must feel or hear the wild beating of her heart?

He reached behind her and she felt the band of her bra slacken. He pushed the straps off the ends of her shoulders and, his mouth still locked with hers, disposed of the bra, leaving no barrier between her soft yielding flesh and the warm solidity of his torso.

Slowly, caressingly, he eased the elastic at the top of her panties over the swell of her behind and pushed them downwards until she had only to part her knees for them to slither to her ankles.

Finally, he ended the kiss and drew back, taking in her nakedness with a look that felt like a sudden rush of hot air on her bare skin.

'You're even more beautiful without your clothes on,' he said huskily.

And then he shed his towel and, briefly, she had a glimpse of his own magnificent, aroused body before he turned away, stepped into the bath and sat down in it.

'Come on in. The water's great,' he said, smiling and holding out his arms in an invitation to join him.

There was no option but to obey. Turning her back to him, Liz stepped over the rim of the bath with one foot then the other. Conscious that he would be getting a head-on view of her backside—'in your face' took on a new meaning here—she bent to put her hands on the bath's sides while lowering herself to sit between his long brown thighs.

Cam's hands on her hips helped her, sliding round to her midriff as he sank back against the bath's sloping end and drew her against him. For the first time in her life she experienced the luxury of leaning against a man's body instead of the unyielding surface of enamelled steel.

It felt wonderful: the difference between the metal type of park bench and the comfort of a feather-cushioned armchair.

'This is where it begins to get really good, don't you think?' he murmured close to her ear.

Not trusting her voice to work normally, Liz nodded her head.

'And it gets better…much better.' One of his hands slid downwards to stroke her stomach and the other moved higher to gently explore her right breast, sending a lightning-flash of exquisite sensation through her.

Then he took the upper hand away. 'I forgot something…'

She felt his stomach muscles contract and harden as he used them to pull himself upwards, lifting her with him to reach for the water controls set in the centre of the long inner side of the bath.

It was only when the water began to bubble and swirl that she realised the bath was equipped with jets that now were sending gentle currents in several directions.

Behind her, Cam relaxed and resumed the gentle exploration of her breast, moving his palm lightly over the part that was reacting to his touch. His other thumb was caressing her navel which suddenly seemed to have become a previously undiscovered erogenous zone.

She heard herself give a long shuddering sigh and, seemingly of their own volition, her hands, which had been lying at the tops of her legs, moved to rest on his longer legs, her fingers spread on the tanned thighs raised at an angle on either side of her.

She heard him say, 'Close your eyes...don't think about anything but how good this is...for both of us.'

She did as he told her, discovering that it intensified her response to his touch. But her inhibitions revived when the hand on her belly suddenly moved down, his long fingers invading the tangle of wet curls at the apex of her thighs, startling her into an instinctive recoil.

'Relax...it's all right...it's fine.'

With that low, calm voice he might have been reassuring a nervous animal; and in a sense she was, she acknowledged. Though it wasn't him she was nervous of, but rather herself, of her own inability to—

The thought was cut short by a wave of intense sensation as his fingers began to explore.

The minutes passed. There was silence except for the murmurous sound of the churning water and her own increasingly laboured breathing. Soon she was lost, her neck arched, her hands gripping his legs, her body convulsed by spasm after delicious spasm against which there was no possible resistance.

When it was over, when his hands were no longer touching her most sensitive places but were merely fondling her shoulders, she became aware of what, overwhelmed by ecstasy, she had temporarily forgotten: the hard ridge of engorged male flesh she could feel pressing against the base of her spine. While she was relaxed, all her tensions released, he was not, or that part of him was not. Yet, despite his palpable lust for her, he wasn't sending out any signals of impatience. How strange! Her experience was that male urges had to be satisfied quickly, not kept waiting. Not that Cam's could be satisfied in a tub that, large though it was, was not *that* large. But he showed no inclination to bring their time in it to an end. He must have exceptional self-control, she thought.

'If you want to nod off, don't mind me,' he said. 'It's been a long action-packed day. Have a mini-*siesta*…do you good.'

She did feel extraordinarily drowsy. As he said, it must be the combined after-effect of this morning's wedding, the flight, the drive from Madrid, the apprehension about their first time in bed together followed by the soothing warmth of the water and the physical release he had given her.

'But what about you?' she murmured.

'Don't worry about me. My turn will come later. This is your time for unwinding…the more unwound you are, the better it will be for us both.'

It was tempting to do as he suggested and slip into a doze, and perhaps she did for a few minutes. Afterwards she wasn't sure whether she had been sleeping when he started caressing her again.

'Oh, Cam…no…please,' she protested.

But he ignored her. The slow build-up of pleasure began again and she let it happen, helpless against those skilful, commanding hands that understood exactly how to undermine her resistance. There was a part of her mind that didn't approve of her capitulation, but her mind wasn't in control, only her senses.

This time the pleasure grew even more intense. Her body tingled and throbbed and she could not stop herself making small ecstatic noises and, at the final moment, a louder sound that she tried to muffle with her hand.

'Anyone listening outside the bathroom door would think I was torturing you,' he said, with amusement in his voice.

In a way he was. She had kept her emotions under wraps for so long that now to abandon all control felt as horrendous as betraying secrets to the enemy.

'Nice as this is, I think we'd better transfer ourselves,' he said. 'If we stay in the bath too long, you'll be getting washerwoman's fingers.'

Pulling himself into a sitting position, and her with him, he gave her a swift kiss on the back of the neck before climbing out. A moment later he was holding a large bath sheet, ready to wrap it round her when she rose from the water and stepped onto the bath mat.

As soon as she was enveloped in the thick soft white pile of the towel, Cam leaned over the bath to turn off the jets and pull out the plug. He was obviously completely at ease with his own body and she envied him his freedom from self-consciousness. But how many other women had seen him like this? she wondered, with a pang, averting her eyes from the sight of his arousal. But not quickly enough to avoid being caught out as he turned and intercepted the direction of her gaze.

After shrugging on his bathrobe, he said, 'Let's go and try out the bed.'

'Shouldn't we dry our feet first?'

His response to this was to put his hands on her shoulders and steer her into a sitting position on the edge of the bath. Then, taking one of the smaller towels, he began to dry her feet for her.

She looked at the dark head bent over her foot and couldn't repress the impulse to stroke his thick glossy hair and let her fingers slide to the back of his brown neck. He didn't look up but she saw his mouth curve in a smile. It encouraged her to obey the urge to lean forward and put her lips to his cheek.

'You're being incredibly nice to me,' she murmured.

'It's not hard.' He kept his mouth straight, but his eyes were amused.

As soon as her other foot was dry, he tossed the towel aside and scooped her into his arms.

Liz had never been carried before, or not since she was small. Cam carried her to the bedroom as easily as if she were a child, not an adult female weighing one hundred and thirty pounds. She found it curiously exciting to be swept off her feet and supported by strong arms around her back and under her knees. It was also, she discovered, a turn-on. It made her feel fragile and helpless, and totally in his power, not a state of mind she would have expected to like—or would have liked with anyone else. But because it was Cam she did.

Earlier, when they had first entered the suite, the bedclothes had been hidden by a spread that matched the curtains at the corners of the bed. Now the spread had vanished, presumably removed by Cam before he started running their bath.

At the side of the bed, he set her on her feet, removing the towel he had wrapped round her and letting it fall on the rug. Then, picking her up, he put her on the bed before walking round to the other side of it, at the same time shedding his robe. A moment later he was stretched out beside her, propped on one elbow while his other hand gently but firmly parted her legs. Stroking the sensitive skin on the insides of her thighs with his fingertips, slowly he bent his head till his mouth was only an inch from her breast and she was holding her breath, knowing that the touch of his lips was going to send a thousand watts of ecstasy shooting through every nerve in her body.

As it did.

It was a long time later, and Liz was lying with closed eyes, exhausted by wave after wave of mind-blowing pleasure, when suddenly Cam was above her and inside her. It happened so smoothly and easily, like a sword sliding into its scabbard, that it took her by surprise. It had never been like this before, but then nothing in her previous experience had been remotely like Cam's way of making love.

Swept by an overwhelming longing to return the heavenly sensations he had given her, she obeyed an instinct to slide her arms round his neck and embrace his hips with her legs. It must have been the right thing to do because, from deep inside his chest, came the same sort of sound he had forced from her in the bath. And then her mind switched off and instinct took over completely.

Before she was fully awake, Liz knew that something extraordinary and life-changing had happened. She opened her eyes and saw, with momentary puzzlement, not a ceiling but the roof of a tent that, seconds later, she recognised as the canopy of the four-poster bed.

Then everything else came back in a rush of vivid memory and, turning her head, she saw, lying beside her, her husband who was now also her lover.

As the details of what they had done together came back, she felt a powerful longing to repeat the experience.

But Cam was asleep, lying on his back with one hand under his head and the other spread on his midriff.

Slowly and carefully, so as not to disturb him, Liz raised herself on her elbow and began a leisurely study of him, starting with his unconscious face and moving slowly down his long relaxed body until she came to the place where the part of him that had fitted so perfectly inside her now lay lax and quiescent among his dark curls, like a slow-worm sleeping in a nest of heather.

There had been so little real intimacy in her previous marriage that she was intensely curious about the transformation from this state to the other. She wanted to see it happen…to make it happen…to give him the same intense long-drawn-out pleasure he had given her.

Impelled by an irresistible urge, she reached out and laid the flat of her hand very lightly on the warm skin below the small hollow of his navel. He did not stir. Encouraged, she slid her fingers across his flat stomach, feeling the underlying muscles that were slack now but could quickly harden as they had in the bath. He continued to sleep, his breathing so deep and slow that he scarcely seemed to be breathing at all.

She leaned over and put her lips to the place where her hand had been, tasting his skin with her tongue while her hand ventured further afield, exploring the foreign territory of a body that was the way a man's body ought to be, lean and powerful and compellingly male.

Who would have thought that a man like this could also be so intuitive about a woman like her beset by so many hang-ups and inhibitions? Gratitude for his patience and understanding welled up inside her. In one day—even one hour—he had given her more pleasure than she would have thought possible in the light of her previous disillusioning experience.

For several minutes she explored, with soft kisses and gentle caresses, every part of his torso except the one she wanted to touch. Then she plucked up her courage and curled her hand lightly round him, ready to snatch it away if he showed signs of waking up. Not that he was likely to mind her exploration, but she hadn't yet reached the point of feeling no shyness with him. Hopefully that would happen as the honeymoon progressed, but this was only the first day.

Cam's body began to respond yet he still seemed soundly asleep. Her confidence growing, she watched the miraculous transformation that her touch was inducing. Why, until now, had she always thought of a man's wedding tackle as ugly, even grotesque, when in fact it was strangely beautiful in its colouring, shape and texture?

I suppose it's because I love him, she thought. Nothing about him disgusts me. Everything about him delights me. But I can never tell him that. This is the only way I can express my feelings.

'Are you trying to tell me something?'

The unexpected question made her jump.

Disconcerted, she said, 'I—I thought you were having a nap.'

His eyes gleamed through half-closed lids. 'I was, but you woke me up...in the nicest possible way.'

As she let go, he captured her hand and replaced it where it had been. 'Don't stop. I like it. I'd like to be woken this way from all my *siestas*.'

Then his shoulders came off the bed and his mouth found hers. Her last coherent thought was that he would never know how close his question had come to the truth.

Most of the *parador's* guests had already assembled in the bar when, a little before nine, Cam and Liz went down to dinner.

After a waiter brought their drinks, Cam lifted his glass to her. Leaning forward and looking into her eyes, he said, '"To me in your arms and you in my room...a door that is locked and a key that is lost...and a night that's a thousand years long".'

His voice was never loud, but a woman sitting nearby, not listening to her elderly husband pontificating to another man, gave Cam a startled look that made Liz want to laugh.

'Is that from a poem?' she asked.

He nodded. 'An anonymous verse in a book of erotic poetry that we'll read together when we get home. Not that I feel we're much in need of inspiration.' He cast an eye round the room and dropped his voice to a level that only she would hear. 'Some of this lot look as if they've forgotten all the pleasures of the flesh except eating.'

'Perhaps they have,' she said, sympathising with them. Until this afternoon she had been in a similar predicament.

The dining room was a lofty mediaeval hall, its stone walls hung with colourful banners. The high-backed chairs were upholstered with crimson velvet and the lamps on the tables had red silk shades.

'If we're going to be here for a week, there's plenty of time to try all these regional specialities,' said Liz, after studying the menu. 'Would you mind if, tonight, I had something light? Having eaten on the plane, and had tea when we arrived, I'm not terribly hungry. But I don't want to stop you feasting.'

'I feel exactly the same,' said Cam. 'What about having some asparagus to start with and then *huevos en conchas*—eggs in scallop shells. They're very light.'

'That sounds perfect.'

After signalling to the head waiter and giving him their order, Cam said, 'Large meals late in the evening are not conducive to ''nights a thousand years long''...or would you rather spend tonight sleeping? As you say, we have plenty of time.'

Whether it was deliberate she couldn't tell, but his tone and the caressing look he gave her made her long to be upstairs, alone with him, instead of down here surrounded by guests and staff.

'Perhaps we shall need to spend some of it sleeping, but not all of it,' she said demurely.

And then she began to laugh because, whatever was wrong with their marriage, there was a lot that was right with it, and here and now—which was what life was really about—she was happy. Very happy.

Cam put his hand over hers. 'A long time ago—I think it was the day you nearly stormed out of my garden because you were nervous that I was planning to seduce you—I wondered how you would look with your eyes sparkling. They're sparkling now.'

She turned her hand to clasp his. 'I think what you're seeing must be what one of my favourite poets called "the lineaments of gratified desire".'

She wondered if he would know which poet she meant and the context of the phrase she had quoted—'In a wife I would desire what in whores is always found—the lineaments of gratified desire'. Cam was a well-read man, but William Blake, the visionary poet and painter, unrecognised in his lifetime, was still not as widely known as she felt he deserved to be.

To her delight, Cam said, 'At school I thought poetry was boring waffle until I read Blake's "Tyger! Tyger! burning bright In the forests of the night, What immortal hand or eye Could frame thy fearful symmetry?"'

Discussing Blake's life and his strange, powerful paintings led them to other subjects that kept them talking until they had finished their meal.

'It's a mild night and there's a full moon. Shall we walk round the gardens?' Cam suggested, as they left the dining room.

Outside the building, he tucked her arm through his and they strolled along the gravel walks in companionable silence until he stopped and said, 'It's a little cooler than I thought. You'd better have my jacket. I don't want you getting chilled.'

He had been shedding his jacket while he was speaking. Now he wrapped it round her and then bent his head to kiss her.

'Maybe it would be a better idea to tour the garden tomorrow,' he said, against her lips. 'Stone seats look romantic but they're not that comfortable to sit on. Upstairs we have a sofa... What do you think?'

'I vote for the sofa,' said Liz, thinking it might not be long before the four-poster bed seemed an even better option.

They had been honeymooning for three days when a courier service delivered the photographs taken outside the register office by a photographer Cam knew who could be relied on to not sell any prints to the press.

Later, studying the pictures in greater detail while Cam was checking his e-mails, as he did once a day, Liz thought that no one would guess that it hadn't been a normal wedding. She was also surprised by how much she had changed since her first in-laws had taken some holidays snaps of her. The woman in the blue suit smiling up at Cam seemed a different person from the one she had been six or seven years ago when the previous snaps had been taken.

*   *   *

On their final morning at the *parador*, they shared the bath for the last time and then dried and went back to bed to make leisurely love.

Later, in the peaceful aftermath, when they were still locked in each other's arms but their hearts were beating at a normal rate, Cam said quietly, close to her ear, 'Have you enjoyed staying here?'

Liz raised her head just enough to press a kiss on the muscular shoulder an inch or two from her mouth. 'Silly question…you know I have. The walks…the food…the views…having nothing to do but relax…it's been perfect.'

Not quite perfect, was her afterthought, but she dismissed it. She was here in his arms, wasn't she?

When, a little later, Cam rolled onto his back and stretched his long frame out beside her, he considered suggesting they should extend their visit. It was tempting to prolong this extraordinarily pleasurable hiatus between the past and the future. As Liz said, the setting was idyllic and the food superb.

One thing she hadn't listed was the great sex they had shared. But he knew that, physically at least, she had enjoyed it as much as he. He had never known anyone more desirable than the woman lying quietly beside him. To look at her was to want her, and it wasn't the kind of desire that quickly wore off because they had other things in common. He liked her mind as much as her lovely body.

But he couldn't forget that, after the first time he had made love to her, she had cried. Still imprisoned in his arms, she must have thought he was dozing, but he had been awake and had known what was happening. Maybe it would have been better to have talked about it. But at the time he had felt it was best to ignore it.

Perhaps that had been a mistake.

On the night they returned to Valdecarrasca, they had dinner with the Drydens.

Greeting Liz with a hug, Leonora said, 'It's a cliché but there's no other word for it...you look radiant, my dear. Cam, too, if radiant can be applied to a man. Was the *parador* wonderful? It's not one I've ever been to.'

'It's a good one,' said Cam. 'But it was my companion who made it special.' The look he gave Liz as he said it was so convincingly lover-like that it crossed her mind he might have been even more successful as an actor than as a TV reporter.

She gave him the sort of smile that was appropriate for a bride when her husband is being gallant. 'Yes, it was a lovely place. Although it was my first experience of a *parador*, I'm sure it has to be one of the best,' she told the Drydens.

The meal Leonora provided was an informal family supper starting with avocados and followed by an earthenware dish of sliced aubergines and peppers topped with cheese and baked in the oven. For pudding they had fresh fruit.

They stayed till about eleven and then walked home to La Higuera with Cam holding her hand as if she were the wife he had always longed for.

At night, in his bedroom, which it would take time to think of as their bedroom, it was easy to delude herself that it was only a matter of time before the illusion of a normal marriage developed into a reality. But downstairs, during the daylight hours, she had moments of acute doubt. Every day her longing to express her feelings in words increased. Sometimes when he touched her in a loving way, she had difficulty not recoiling from the caress because what she really wanted was for him to tell her he loved her.

But how could he tell her that, when it wasn't true? She was wishing for the moon and she knew it. Love wasn't part of their bargain. She knew she should be content with what she had:

a beautiful home and an expert lover who had already given her hours of physical pleasure.

You can't have everything, she told herself. But, as much as living at La Higuera delighted her, she would have swapped it for a tumbledown *casita* on a mountainside, with water drawn from a well and primitive sanitation, to hear Cam say those three little words.

Cam was beginning to feel there was a ghost in his house: the spectre of a man who, although he had ended his life heroically, didn't sound as if he had been a ball of fun while he was alive. Neither of Liz's first husband's interests, coin-collecting and watching sport on TV, were activities that appealed to him. He found spectator sports boring and, at school, had never distinguished himself playing team games though he had enjoyed ski-ing and canoeing.

It had always been his impression that hogging the TV remote control, and spending hours glued to football and cricket matches, were minuses rather than pluses when women were rating male behaviour. But it seemed that Liz had accepted these shortcomings where Duncan was concerned.

Cam also suspected that she wasn't wholly comfortable with the excellence of their own sexual relationship. She enjoyed it while it was

happening but, when they were not in bed together, he had the feeling she experienced powerful guilt feelings, as if she had betrayed a trust.

How long was Duncan's ghost going to haunt
her…haunt them both? he wondered.

In theory, as long as their marriage was working according to the terms agreed, he should
have been satisfied. But somehow he wasn't. He
wanted her to be happy…happier than she was.
He had no emotional baggage from the past, and
it irked him that she had…might always have.

One afternoon when Cam was working on an
article he had been commissioned to contribute
to an influential magazine, Liz went down to her
house to sort through her drawers and cup-
boards. She had more or less decided to put the
house on the market and invest whatever price
it fetched.

Among the things she came across was the
album of photographs of her first wedding and
another album of snapshots of herself and
Duncan taken in their teens and twenties.

I don't need to keep these, she thought. They
record a part of my life that is better laid to rest.
Or perhaps I should send some of them to
Duncan's parents. They have a duplicate of the
wedding album but they may not have some of
the other pictures of him.

Going through them, taking out the photographs she thought her first in-laws might not have copies of, she came to a studio portrait of Duncan that before their engagement had lived in the drawer of her bedside table and, afterwards, had been framed to stand on her dressing table. It showed him in the suit he had bought for job interviews, his hair cut in the style of the time, a slightly self-conscious smile on his face.

She thought of the hours she had spent gazing at features that had seemed to her then to embody every masculine virtue and charm. How different they looked to her now. Her eyes misted, her lips quivered, and tears brimmed over and trailed down her cheeks.

It was at that moment that the front door opened and Cam walked in. 'Hi…how are you getting on?' he asked, closing the door behind him. 'I've finished the draft of my piece. Later I'll get you to read it…see what you think.'

Then he saw her fumbling for a tissue and, when she couldn't find one, wiping her cheeks with her fingers.

'Liz…darling…what's wrong?'

He produced a man-sized tissue and gave it to her, his expression concerned. Even in her dismay at being caught having a foolish weep, she registered the 'darling'. He had never called her that before.

Cam noticed what she was holding and took it from her. 'Who's this? Need I ask? Duncan.'

As he studied his predecessor, she saw a range of reactions reflected in his face, the first unwilling curiosity being quickly replaced by a look of disdain, as if he could see at a glance what had taken her a long time to recognise.

Then, as he tossed the photograph on top of the pile of others, his face became a mask of anger she had never seen him wear before.

'For God's sake,' he blazed at her, 'are you going to spend the rest of your life in mourning? He's been dead for four years. Whatever you shared with him is over and done with. You're *my* wife now. It's not right to be down here, mooning over the past.'

'I wasn't mooning,' she protested. 'You don't understand.'

'No, I bloody well don't! It's time you snapped out of it. Life moves on and, if we have any sense, we move with it. We may not have married for the conventional reasons, but now that's all changed. I love you...and you could love me if you tried...if you put your mind to it...if you stopped mourning him.'

She sprang to her feet. 'What do you mean...you love me? You've never said so.'

'Well, I'm saying it now.' He sounded more enraged than loving. 'I didn't expect to fall in love with you, but I have…and I want you to love me…not him—' with a glare at the topmost photo.

'I never loved him.'

For the first time she said aloud the truth that for years she had chosen not to acknowledge because facing it had been more painful than living a lie.

'You never loved him?' Cam repeated. But now it was a question, not a statement.

'It was calf love…not the real thing. I realised that on our honeymoon,' she said, in a low voice. 'It was so different from ours…you can't begin to imagine. You are everything that he wasn't…tender…unselfish…imaginative. That first night at the *parador* was like being led into paradise after years in purgatory.' She gave a long uneven sigh. 'The only remaining torment was not being able to tell you I loved you. Do you *really* love me? Do you mean it?'

For answer he pulled her into his arms and gripped her so tightly she thought her ribs might crack. But after a moment or two he relaxed and adjusted his hold.

'I must be as thick as two planks,' he said, speaking into her hair. 'I've been falling in love with you for months, but I didn't recognise the symptoms. I knew that you were everything I wanted and needed in a woman, and I knew I was as jealous as hell of your first husband, but I didn't put two and two together. How stupid can a guy be?'

He drew back slightly and tilted her face up to his. 'Liz…sweet, lovely Liz…what a dumbo you've married.'

And then he kissed her with a tenderness that was both familiar and novel because now, at last, there were no secrets between them.

One kiss led to another and presently Cam picked her up and carried her up the stairs to her bedroom, where they tore off their clothes and made eager love on the unmade bed, their caresses accompanied by many whispers of 'I love you' and other passionate endearments.

Afterwards they both slept for a little while, waking at the same time to smile into each other's eyes, luxuriating in this new and wonderful harmony that flowed between them like an invisible current.

Presently, Liz said, 'Would you like a cup of tea?'

Cam burst out laughing. 'A houri and a housewife rolled into one. What more can any man ask for? Yes, I'd love a cup of tea, dearest girl, but let's go home and have it there.'

Later, when they were sitting in the sun near the fig tree, watching and listening to the bees at work in the lavender bushes, he said, 'If you were unhappy with Duncan, why didn't you leave him?'

It took her some moments to answer. Eventually, she said, 'I had promised to be his wife "for better or worse". If you make that commitment, I think you should try to stick to it...as long as there is no cruelty or infidelity involved, which there wasn't in our case. Anyway Duncan *was* happy. In his way, he loved me. He didn't deserve to be left in the lurch...and he couldn't keep up the mortgage without my contribution.' She sighed. 'It's a long story. Do you really want to hear it?'

'Very much...I want to know everything about you.'

'Duncan was the boy next door. I had a crush on him from about the age of fourteen. By the time I was seventeen I was fathoms deep in love...or thought I was. What did I know...what does anybody know about love at that age? If he hadn't been interested in me, or if either of us had left home and seen a bit of the world, it would have worn off—no harm done.'

'But he was interested in you?'

'Yes, and our parents encouraged us. Legally, of course, they couldn't have stopped us marrying when I was nineteen. But they could and should have done more to make us see sense and wait. I'm sure there are people who mature early and marry young and it works out. But we weren't among them.'

'You said earlier that you realised that on your honeymoon. You were a virgin, obviously. Was he?'

'I'm not certain about that. I asked him, but he was evasive. If he had had any previous experience, it hadn't taught him anything. He was like someone who's colour blind or has no ear for music. He had no instinctive understanding of what sexual love is about. I knew it might hurt the first time, but it went on hurting for weeks and months.'

'Wham, bam, thank you, ma'am?'

Cam's query brought a faint smile to her mouth. 'Exactly. I knew all the theory and I tried to get it across that he...we weren't going about things the right way.'

'But he resented any suggestion that he wasn't the world's best lover?'

'How did you guess?'

'The world is full of guys who can't take any criticism of their driving let alone their technique in bed. Did you try giving him a book on the subject?'

'Yes, but it didn't work. Duncan was strangely prudish in lots of ways…I think he got it from his mother. We always had sex on Wednesdays and Saturdays, and always in the dark.' For the first time she was able to laugh about it with genuine amusement and no tightening of the throat.

'*Dios mio!*' said Cam. 'What an idiot.' They had been sitting close but not actually touching. Now he put his arm round her and pulled her against him. 'I'm amazed you could stand it.'

'Sometimes I wondered that. It wasn't just our disastrous sex life…we had nothing in common. Different senses of humour. Different views about life. But I don't think that's so unusual. Every time you go to a restaurant you see couples with nothing to say to each other, lost in their separate thoughts instead of chatting and laughing.'

'So it wasn't grief you were feeling when I saw that look in your eyes that I took to be sadness?'

'I expect it was guilt because I wasn't able to grieve for him. Or it may have been worry because, for a long time, I thought I was in the grip of another infatuation—for you. I was worried that I was falling into the same trap again.'

She snuggled against him, leaning her head on his shoulder. 'I had got it into my head that a man with such powerful sexual magnetism had to be a worthless person—or at least rather second-rate.'

'It was unfortunate that we met when I had a girlfriend in tow,' he said dryly. 'I could tell that put you off. There were strong vibes of disapproval.'

'The night you arrived I saw you kissing her through that window,' she said, pointing to it. 'I wasn't sure who you were then and I remember envying her because no one was ever going to hold me and kiss me like that.'

'You were wrong there. Someone is going to hold you and kiss you every day for the next forty years...longer with any luck. Shall I open a bottle of wine?'

'Why not?' she said happily.

'Sit tight. I won't be long.' He rose from the seat, then bent to drop a kiss on her forehead. Going up the steps to the upper terrace, he blew her some more kisses.

Liz returned them, wondering how long the impasse between them might have continued if he hadn't found her in tears and thought she was weeping for Duncan rather than over her own youthful folly.

How difficult it was to see into people's hearts if they had reasons for concealing their innermost feelings, she thought.

When he came back with glasses and an opened bottle of white wine in a plastic cooler, she said, 'When did you know you loved me?'

'I'd have to think about that. Men aren't continually analysing their emotions the way women seem to,' he said teasingly. Then, more seriously, 'Perhaps I knew from the beginning that you were someone special but I didn't want to acknowledge it. When you've been independent for years, it's hard to adjust to the fact that you've lost that autonomy...that someone else is in charge of your happiness.'

After a pause he added, 'After the first time I made love to you, you cried. You thought I was dozing, but I could feel your chest heaving. That worried me a lot.'

Remembering the tears she had fought to control, she said, 'If I'd had any sense I'd have had a big boo-hoo, and you'd have asked why, and I would have told you. It was only relief and happiness because, at long last, I'd felt all the things women are supposed to feel.'

'I thought you were probably crying from some kind of guilt about experiencing pleasure without any deep emotional engagement, or from a feeling that you had betrayed the memory of the man you had loved,' said Cam. 'I took it as read that your first marriage had been happy, and from that basic misconception drew a lot of other false conclusions.'

'What I didn't…still don't understand is why you held off from trying me out, bedwise, before taking me on as a wife,' said Liz. 'If you had been a shy man, awkward with women, it might have made sense. But for Valdecarrasca's notorious womaniser to hold back seemed very peculiar.'

'I guess the answer to that is that Valdecarrasca's notorious womaniser had found the woman he wanted for the rest of his life and was nervous of putting a foot wrong. I hadn't recognised my own condition. I thought you'd agreed to our marriage mainly to have some babies. Since getting it right in bed can sometimes take time, it seemed wise to postpone it until we were past the point of no return.'

A few days later, Liz returned from accompanying Leonora to choose a frame for the portrait to see, from the kitchen window, Cam sitting in the garden reading a letter, more mail on the seat beside him.

After filling two tall glasses with spring water they had collected from one of the many *fontanales* to be found in the countryside, she went out to join him.

'Anything for me?'

'Not today, babe.' He stood up to kiss her, then moved the pile of shrink-wrapped magazines and manila envelopes to make room for her to sit next to him. 'How did the session with the framer go?'

'Fine. We found something we both like and I'm sure you will too.' She could see that his thoughts were elsewhere. 'Anything exciting in your post?'

Cam gave her a look she found hard to interpret. For a moment it took her back to the time when neither of them had understood the other. But that was over: now they understood every nuance of each other's tones and expressions. Or so she had thought.

He said slowly, 'I've been asked to step into the shoes of one of Britain's top journalists in Washington DC. He died a couple of weeks ago after working there for twenty years. He was a giant among journalists. It's a huge compliment to be invited to take his place.'

Something his mother had said at the pre-wedding party echoed in her mind. *I hope you know what you're letting yourself in for... You will never enjoy any sense of permanence.*

She said, 'That's wonderful news. When do you have to start? If they want you immediately, I can close up the house and follow you later.'

He was visibly astonished. 'You can't be serious? You love it here. You don't want to leave.'

'I wouldn't want to go back where I came from, but the chance to live in America—that's different. Valdecarrasca won't go away. It will always be here for us.'

Cam swallowed the rest of the water and then sprang to his feet and started pacing back and forth. 'I don't know…it's not what we planned. Washington is a big city and I'd need to live in the centre.'

'If it's one of the pinnacles of a career in journalism, I think you should at least try it. If you don't, you'll always regret it.'

He came back to where she was sitting and crouched down in front of her, putting his hands over her knees. 'But what about you, darling girl? We're a partnership now. We have to consider what's right for us both. If, in a few months' time, you find that you're pregnant, wouldn't you rather be here in the village than in a capital city on the other side of the Atlantic?'

Liz was beginning to think that she might be pregnant already. Her period, normally punctual to the day, was three days overdue and none of her usual mild PM symptoms had materialised.

'I think for someone of my age, having a first baby, Washington might have advantages over provincial Spain. Medical care in the US is said to be second to none—as long as people can afford it. Here…I'm not really sure. I've heard some excellent reports and I've also heard horror stories. Anyway, that's not the crux of the matter. The crux is…if you want to go, I'll be happy to come with you.' Leaning forward, she rested her forearms on his broad shoulders. 'There are thousands of places in the world where I could enjoy living. But only one man I want to live with…and who wants to live with me.'

The most important decision was not the only one. There were many lesser decisions to make.

Later that day, Cam said, 'I don't much like the idea of other people living at La Higuera, but it doesn't make sense to leave it empty for several years, particularly as, under Spanish law, tax is payable on the theoretical letting value.'

'What about storing all your most personal possessions next door?' Liz suggested. 'It would be awful to come back and find that a tenant's obnoxious child had thrown a dart at the portrait of Captain Fielding, or ruined one of your rugs.'

Throughout the house the floors were spread with rugs he had bought on his travels.

'*Our* rugs,' he corrected her. 'Hopefully the letting agency will make sure nobody with obnoxious children is allowed near the place. But that's a good idea. We can use your little house as a store.'

'*Our* little house,' she teased him.

He pulled her into his arms. 'Houses... possessions...they're all expendable,' he said, hugging her. 'That you are mine and I am yours is the only thing that really matters.'

On their last morning in Spain, Liz went to the bakery for bread. On the way home she made a detour, climbing the path that led up to the cemetery and passed behind it to join a flight of rough stone steps leading downwards.

At the top of the steps she paused to look down on the clustered rooftops of Valdecarrasca and, beyond them, the vineyards spreading across the floor of the valley. Between some of the rows of vines the coppery soil had been rotavated. Some were still green with the foliage of low-growing plants. Either way, from this height, the vines themselves looked like rows of cross-stitch worked with varying degrees of skill.

I am going to miss it, she thought. I wonder how long it will be before we come back?

She was certain now that she had started a baby. But she hadn't mentioned it to Cam yet and, observant as he was, he had been too pre-occupied with the preparations for departure to register that they had been making love without any marked interruption since they were married.

Perhaps she would tell him on the flight from Madrid to Washington. Or perhaps she would wait until her instinctive feeling that there was a new life beginning inside her body had been confirmed by a doctor.

She began to descend the steps, wondering if Valdecarrasca would have changed by the time they saw it again. She hoped not. To her, it was perfect as it was, a backwater set apart from the turbulent mainstream of modern life.

Part of her longed to stay, to see the young leaves starting to sprout on the vines and, as the nights grew warmer, to have candlelit suppers for friends in the courtyard. There were also small improvements she wanted to make to the house and garden.

But she hadn't forgotten that on the day he had proposed to her Cam had said that a successful marriage was an intimate friendship between people prepared to make trade-offs.

For the amazing difference he had made to her life, she was more than willing to make this particular trade-off.

Cam must have seen her coming down the steps from the kitchen window. He was at the door to meet her. 'I was beginning to wonder what had happened to you.'

'What could happen to me here?' she said, smiling.

'Nothing, I guess.' He drew her into the house, took the bread bag from her and hung it from the curlicue at the end of the staircase handrail in order to have both hands free to draw her to him. 'I get a little jumpy when you're gone for longer than I expected. Hopefully it will wear off after we've been together twenty or thirty years.'

She wrapped her arms round him. 'I was saying goodbye to the village.'

He tipped up her chin. 'You're sad to be leaving it, aren't you?'

'Only a little...aren't you?'

'There'll be times when I'll miss it. We both will. But the village will always be here for us, and you're going to like America.'

His kiss dispelled her regret for all they were leaving. Since the beginning of history women had been following men to the ends of the earth, saying goodbye to the safe and familiar and setting out on adventures in faraway places.

She had done it before, on her own. If she hadn't, she wouldn't be in the arms of this man she loved and who loved her.

When the kiss ended, she said, 'You're right. It's going to be fun. So let's have breakfast and get on with closing down the house. I wonder how long it will be before someone rents it?'

MILLS & BOON® PUBLISH EIGHT LARGE PRINT TITLES A MONTH. THESE ARE THE EIGHT TITLES FOR JULY 2002

———— ❦ ————

THE SECRET LOVE-CHILD
Miranda Lee

AN ARABIAN MARRIAGE
Lynne Graham

THE SPANIARD'S SEDUCTION
Anne Mather

THE GREEK TYCOON'S BRIDE
Helen Brooks

THE BOSS'S DAUGHTER
Leigh Michaels

THE BABY QUESTION
Caroline Anderson

HIS SECRETARY'S SECRET
Barbara McMahon

A SPANISH HONEYMOON
Anne Weale

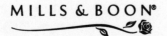

MILLS & BOON®

MILLS & BOON® PUBLISH EIGHT LARGE PRINT TITLES A MONTH. THESE ARE THE EIGHT TITLES FOR AUGUST 2002

THE SHEIKH'S CHOSEN WIFE
Michelle Reid

THE BLACKMAIL BABY
Penny Jordan

THE PREGNANT MISTRESS
Sandra Marton

TO MARRY McKENZIE
Carole Mortimer

THE BRIDE PRICE
Day Leclaire

HIS PRETEND MISTRESS
Jessica Steele

A CONVENIENT WEDDING
Lucy Gordon

THE NANNY'S SECRET
Grace Green

MILLS & BOON®